BACKSHOOTER

Sheriff Ross leaned forward in his seat and glanced across his desk at Spencer. The lawman seemed to be practicing his technique of boring into the person he was interrogating. His puffy face shifted in grimaces of agitation as he asked questions and listened to answers, but his pale blue eyes held steady.

"Your friends don't have very good luck," he said.

"It was his bad luck to be wearing my coat," replied Spencer, "but the shooting itself was no accident. It was planned, same as it was with Collins Wingate."

The sheriff pushed out his lower lip. "You think the same man did both of 'em?"

"I don't know, but it's likely. Same style. Shoot 'em in the back."

"There's a couple of differences," said the sheriff.

"Bound to be some."

"For one thing," continued the sheriff, "you and two others found Wingate. But in this case, there was no one else around but you. . . ."

JOHN D. NESBITT

Not a Rustler

LEISURE BOOKS   NEW YORK CITY

for Deke Latham

A LEISURE BOOK®

February 2010

Dorchester Publishing Co., Inc.
200 Madison Avenue
New York, NY 10016

ISBN 10: 0-8439-6288-7
ISBN 13: 978-0-8439-6288-8
E-ISBN: 978-1-4285-0804-0

The name "Leisure Books" and the stylized "L" with design are trademarks of Dorchester Publishing Co., Inc.

Printed in the United States of America.

10 9 8 7 6 5 4 3 2 1

Visit us online at www.dorchesterpub.com.

Not a Rustler

Chapter One

Spencer Prescott reined his horse to a stop when he saw a rider come over a hill on the trail ahead. The man was leaning forward and had his horse let out at a gallop, leaving a low cloud of dust in his wake.

Spencer moved his horse off to the side of the trail and waited. The oncoming horse was a common-looking sorrel, rigged for ranch work, and the man aboard, in addition to his intent posture, had the appearance of a seasoned range rider. His clothes were dusty, creased, and worn-looking in the sun.

As the man brought the horse to a jolting halt, Spencer recognized the upturned hat brim, the blond mustache, and the hard cheekbones of Kent Anderson, one of the men who rode for George Farrow. The rider worked his reins to each side as the horse, heaving deep breaths, shifted its feet and settled down.

"What news?" called Spencer.

"Nothing good." Sunk into the flushed, sun-weathered face, the man's blue eyes showed alarm. His chest moved up and down. "Someone's killed the boss," he announced.

Spencer felt his pulse jump. "When did that happen?"

Anderson's voice quavered. "This morning, it looks like. He sent us hands out to gather horses. We left at first daylight and come back about noon. Looked like he'd been dead a few hours."

"Right there at the ranch?"

"As he stepped out the front door. Hadn't even pulled it shut."

Spencer shook his head, slow and thoughtful. "That doesn't sound good at all. Any idea who might have done it?"

Anderson gave a hard stare, and his eyes showed bloodshot. "Your guess is as good as mine." He paused, as if to let the comment sink in. Then he went on to say, "You know as well as I do that anyone who isn't part of the Association gets called a rustler and is liable to show up on a list somewhere."

Spencer thought it sounded like an exaggeration, but he said, "I'm sorry for that."

The upturned brim and the drooping blond mustache moved back and forth in an agitated motion, and Spencer couldn't tell if it was from anger or fear.

With another heave of the chest, Anderson spoke. "Nothing personal to you, Spence. You ride for wages just like I do. But you know damn well, what they do to one man, they can do to another. Brand him a rustler, and take it from there. Now, you, you work for a member, so you're on the safe side. For right now."

Spencer frowned. "You think it would come around to me?"

"Oh, hell, who knows? I was thinkin' of myself and the other two boys. If the big cattlemen put it out that George was rustlin', then it's a short step from there to say that the men who ride for him are doin' the same thing. And it could happen to anyone, if the big shots had a mind to do it."

"Well, I sure don't have a part in it."

"Oh, I didn't think you did, or I wouldn't have said this much."

Spencer nodded and said nothing.

Anderson lifted his rein hand from the saddle horn. Worry showed in the blue eyes now. "Well, I've got to get along. I don't like to be the one to do it, but someone's got to carry the news to town."

"Good luck." Spencer raised his hand in farewell.

"Same to you." The upturned brim leaned forward as the rider touched a spur to the horse's flank, and the sorrel with three white stockings moved out in a rising trail of dust.

Spencer shifted in the saddle and nudged his horse forward. The dun stepped into a fast walk, and as Spencer settled into the rhythm, rocking in the smooth leather of the saddle, he went back through the news he had just heard. George Farrow was dead, shot down in his own ranch yard. Spencer recalled an image of Farrow—a quiet, dark-featured man with deep-set eyes and a bushy mustache. Now he was lying on his back, his eyes closed forever. His men would have taken him inside and laid him out with his hands folded on his chest, with his hat on a chair nearby.

Spencer brushed away some of the dust that had settled on his eyelids and cheekbones. He felt the warmth of the sun on his back, the energy of springtime as the grass was growing out and life was coming back to the rangeland. Raising his eyes to scan the country around him, he took a long breath and thought about the man who would not be able to see it anymore.

It was a bad way to go, even if Farrow had branded a few slick calves, which he might have done. Turnabout was supposed to be fair play, at least when it came to branding strays. The way Spencer had seen things in the last few years, everyone lost a few and picked up a few, and so it all came out even. That was the way things went on the open range. But now the men who ran the Association wanted to do things their way, and their way only. Cattlemen whose men mavericked through the winter, as Spencer had done for five dollars a head, wanted to outlaw anyone who didn't participate in the Association's roundups. Even a man who was branding his own stock could be called a rustler, while the Association kept all the mavericks in their gather so they could divvy up the proceeds among themselves.

Spencer tried not to concern himself with things that went on in higher-up places. A man who worked for a living liked to think that the man he rode for was on the square. As for branding stray calves or killing a steer that had wandered too far from its own range, those seemed to be common practice. Al Jerome had never asked his men to change a brand or slaughter someone else's beef for sale. He had just followed the custom of the country. If he was a member of the Wyoming Stockgrowers Association, as he was, that was his business, and it helped protect his interests. As Spencer saw it, the bigwig politics didn't reach down to the cowhand's level. Besides, a man needed to work somewhere, and most of the good work was with men like Al Jerome.

Meanwhile, George Farrow was dead, shot down, and his hired man Anderson blamed the big ranchers. He made a point of saying he didn't hold it against another ranch hand, but Spencer was left feeling uneasy. He felt the man's bitterness, and he knew how the elite cattlemen hung together. Still, he was not going to jump to conclusions. He was in a position to stay calm and keep his eyes and ears open. Then, if he didn't like the look of things, he could ease out and go look for work somewhere else.

Spencer had another fleeting image of George Farrow laid out, eyes closed, hatless, his weathered complexion fading into the pale forehead and tousled hair. He would never again see this greening rangeland, never again feel the warmth of the sun as the country came out of winter. Anderson said it could happen to anyone.

He also said Spencer's guess was as good as his, and he didn't mean all guesses were possible. It was clear that he meant there was one good guess if a man chose not to ignore it.

Talk of the killing had reached the A-J Ranch by the time Spencer rode in and put his horse away. As he took his place at the supper table, he gathered that the other hands had heard the same sketchy details as he had. At the moment, the talk dwelt upon Farrow himself and why he might have come to misfortune.

Al Jerome, boss of the A-J, sat in his customary place, facing the door. He had both hands on the table in front of him, touching a coffee cup with the thumb and first two fingers of each hand. His reddish brown hair caught the glow of lamplight from overhead, and his pointed, upturned nose reminded Spencer, as it sometimes did in certain postures, of a fox. Now with his head lifted and turned, Jerome listened to the talk coming from the table at his left.

A hired man named Waltman said, "If he got into trouble, it was probably of his own makin'."

Spencer was struck by the man's tone, which carried no sympathy. Waltman was not a foreman, but he assumed rank over several of the other hands, and Spencer was accustomed to his comments delivered with an air of authority. At present, though, he seemed to go beyond that point, as if he wanted to disparage the dead man.

As silence hung in the air for a moment, Spencer observed Waltman. The man sat with his forearms resting full-length on the table, his shoulders squared, and his chest high. Settled on his thick neck was a head that Spencer assumed took the largest-sized hat of all those in the bunkhouse. Like the others at the table, he wore no hat at the moment. His short, thick, coarse hair, somewhere between blond and light brown, thatched his top. He had a rough complexion, with little pocks and large pores, so that the face had a full, almost swollen appearance. That, along with large ears and a round nose of corresponding size, and a tendency to squint, made his eyes look small. He was not lethargic, though—just complacent when he had his say—and he gave Spencer the impression of a full-grown tomcat that has lived around a steady source of mice.

Al Jerome broke the silence. "Not sure what you might mean by that, Dick."

Waltman cocked his large head. "I don't know it about him, par-say, but when a small operator has a fast-growing herd, his outfit has likely got long ropes and fast horses. That gets 'em in trouble."

Al Jerome raised his eyebrows. "Well, now, a man doesn't want to be too quick about saying another man's a—"

"Rustler," said Waltman. "And I didn't say he was. I just said that's what men like him some-times get it for."

A young fellow, Perkins, new to the outfit, spoke up. "One man brandin' another's stock. I thought they had to catch him red-handed. Did they do that?"

Jerome answered, "Things aren't the way they used to be. Not with what they call rustling, or with what they do about it." He looked around the table, taking in those men who had stayed on through the winter.

Spencer remembered the man's assurance, back on those cold days when snow lay on the ground. Branding a few mavericks wasn't really rustling, the boss had said. Not like those other fellows did. But winter was over now, and the crew was no longer a small, confidential circle. There were more men on the range in general as well, more eyes and ears, and talk was looser. In the boss's words, there seemed to be an unspoken message that the past was past, and for the present no one should get out of line.

Waltman spoke again. "To answer your question, Perk, I don't know who shot him, or how or why, so I don't know what they had on him."

Spencer frowned and said nothing, but he thought Waltman as much as said that someone had something on Farrow.

"Oh," said the kid. "From the way you talked, I thought maybe you knew something I didn't."

"Everyone knows somethin' that the next man doesn't."

"Isn't that the truth?" said Jerome, with his assuring smile. "Thing is, what a man knows is usually trivial. And I'm speakin' for myself. Everybody's got a headful of knowledge that he acquired without trying and will probably never use—thimbles and barnyard geese and where the post office is in Omaha. Harmless stuff. Why, Perk, if someone pumped you, they'd probably be amazed at all the things you knew and weren't even aware of."

The kid smiled. "I don't know where the post office is in Omaha, but I can tell you where to find it in Canton, Ohio."

"My point exactly. And Dick, here, could tell us where to buy a thimble."

"Small chance of that," said Waltman. "The women I've known don't put their fingers in those things." He gave a wag of the head. "But ask me where they pawn their jewelry and watches, and I can tell you of a couple of places in St. Louis."

***

Spencer reached forward and patted the buckskin on the neck. The horse had shed all his winter hair, and the undercoat felt smooth and warm
to the touch. Sometimes in the morning the buckskin was rambunctious and had to be held in, but
today he felt calm as he stepped out at an even
pace.

According to his assignment that morning,
Spencer was to ride north and then west, which
meant he would go around the Wingate place before he angled off to the range he was supposed to
check on. As he rode north in the gentle warmth
of the sun, he felt in no hurry. He could ride fast
later on if he had to, but right now he was turning
over a couple of thoughts.

About three miles north of the A-J headquarters,
he came to a place where the trail from the west
made a T with the trail he was following. Casting
a glance off to the west, he thought it would not
lengthen his ride by much if he spent a few minutes visiting with Collins Wingate. Spencer gave
a shrug, then turned his horse to the left, and with
the sun warming his back he headed in the direction of Wingate's little place.

After a mile he came to a boundary line that
Wingate had plowed around his quarter-section
claim. For many homesteaders, that was a first
step toward proving up. Some didn't go much
further than that and putting up a sod house, but
Wingate was more industrious. He had a good
water hole to protect on his claim, and as the
neighbors were all aware, he planned to run a
barbed-wire fence all the way around his property line. Meanwhile, he ran cattle on the open

range as everyone else did, and he did not fence in the water hole itself. All the same, everyone knew the larger fence was coming, and no one could deny him the right to put it up and cut off a good water hole from everyone else's cattle.

Spencer let his eye rove out to follow the boundary line. He could imagine the fence all too well, and the thought of it kicked up a little resistance inside him. In spite of his range rider's prejudice, though, he liked Wingate and was interested in knowing what the man might have to say about recent developments. Spencer nudged the buckskin and picked up a fast walk.

Half a mile from the boundary line, the horse and rider topped a small rise. Ahead on the right lay the small house and the stable next to it. No sounds came from the ranch yard or the corrals behind, and a thread of gray smoke rose from the stovepipe sticking out of the roof of the house.

As Spencer rode into the yard, the front door opened. Collins Wingate stood in the doorway, wearing his hat as if he were on his way out, but he stayed in place and raised his head in acknowledgment of his visitor.

"Go ahead and tie him up, and come on in," he said. "There's still coffee."

Spencer swung down, tied the buckskin to the hitching rail, and walked to the doorstep. As he shook hands with Wingate, he took in a quick impression.

The man was dressed as if for work, in a dull white work shirt, brown vest, and denim trousers. He was clean-shaven as usual, and his light brown hair was neat and trimmed. Although his face carried a tenseness, he raised his brows and gave a faint smile.

"Come in," he said, moving aside to let the visitor pass through.

It was the first time Spencer had been inside the house, and he did not see anyone else as he stepped into the front room. The smell of coffee and cooked food, something like flapjacks, hung in the air, and the house had a cozy warmth to it. Spencer turned toward Wingate, who closed the door and stood with an air of hesitation.

"Didn't know if I'd catch you at home," Spencer offered.

"I was on my way out a little earlier, and one of George Farrow's men came by. I guess you heard about what happened."

"I met up with one of his men yesterday afternoon. The one called Anderson."

Wingate nodded, still in a pause. He was a square-built fellow, and his work-roughened hands seemed to be hanging idle at his sides, as if he wanted to do something but didn't know what. "Here," he said, as his brown eyes flickered away and came back, "let's sit down. Eva's in the kitchen. I don't think you've met her. This thing caught us both off guard." He raised his voice. "Say, Eva. We've got another visitor. Come out for a minute when you can." Wingate pointed to a table against the left wall, off to the side of an open doorway, and moved toward it.

Spencer heard the sound of a door closing on a wood stove, and as he was halfway to the table, a woman appeared in the doorway. He stopped and took off his hat.

The woman was of average height, with dark hair and blue eyes. She wore a gray dress and an apron over it, but it was easy to see that she had the pleasant build of a woman who had not yet been worn down by ranch work and childbearing. She had a calm air about her, but she held her hands clasped at the drawn waist of her apron.

"Eva," said Wingate. "This is Spencer Prescott. I think I've mentioned him. Spencer, this is my wife, Eva."

The woman nodded but did not release her hands, so Spencer held his hat in both hands and made a slight bow of the head in return.

"Pleased to meet you, Mrs. Wingate."

"And likewise."

As she turned and went back into the kitchen, Spencer noticed that her hair was tied up in a neat coil. From there his gaze moved to the table, where Wingate was pulling out a chair. The man set his hat on the table and sat down.

Spencer took the closest chair to him, which sat around the corner and perpendicular to Wingate's. A few seconds later, the woman reappeared with a black enamel coffeepot and two cups. No one spoke as she poured the coffee. When she had gone back into the kitchen, Wingate cleared his throat.

"There's nothing good about this," he began.

Spencer shook his head. "Not at all."

"I don't know how much you heard at the place where you work." Wingate held his gaze steady, in a gesture of inviting a comment.

"Not much. Some surprise. Jerome and Waltman were sort of matter-of-fact about it."

"I wouldn't expect them to have much sympathy."
Spencer shook his head, slower this time.

"Well, I'm not trying to get anything out of you. I know you've got a living to make, and I don't want to say anything you wish you hadn't heard."

"Oh, I'm not that easily offended. That fellow Anderson already gave me an idea of how the little man might see it. If I didn't want to know more, or if I was afraid of what I might hear, I wouldn't have come by. On the contrary, I was interested in knowing what it looked like to you."

Wingate raised his brows and gave a close, appraising look. "You want to know what I think?"

"Yes, I do."

As if deciding whether to speak his mind or not, Wingate blew steam across the top of his cup and took a sip of coffee. After a few seconds, he spoke. "Here it is, then. I think these big cattlemen have gotten way too much nerve. I'm not mentioning any names, just saying, some people in general."

"I understand that."

Wingate paused as he looked at his cup.

"Go ahead," said Spencer. "None of this goes beyond here." He waved his hand at the nearby walls. "And there may be something I need to know."

The other man heaved out a breath. "Well, like I say, I think some of these men have gotten the idea that they can do as they wish. They've seen others get away with it, and they think they can do the same."

"Others. . ."

"Ever since they hanged that woman and her common-law partner over on the Sweetwater.

In plain daylight, with witnesses, and they got away with it clean. Then a similar bunch put their heads together and went into it in a bigger way, over in the Powder River country, just last year. And none of them has had to answer to it. Now it seems like some others around here have got the same bold idea."

"Which way? Those men on the Sweetwater took it into their own hands, while the ones up by Casper brought in a bunch of would-be gunmen from Texas."

"That's right. They hired it done. But before they brought in that gang and killed the two men at the K.C., they had someone doin' individual jobs. A back-shooter. When he couldn't get Nate Champion by himself, the bosses brought in their little army. But when he worked on his own, he got some jobs done. Men saw him, and still he got away with it. Even now, it's not healthy to mention his name."

"And you think that's the style someone wants to go in for, or has already gone in for, around here?"

Wingate narrowed his eyes and lowered his voice. "You know this fella named Fred Carlton, the one they call Wolf?"

Spencer moistened his lips, which felt dry. "I know of him. They say he's a stock detective. He's been around here since the middle of winter."

"That's him. He's a stock detective, all right. He doesn't have cattle himself, but he attaches himself to men who do—men of prestige—and he's willing to do their dirty work. He's the kind that's well fitted for it."

"You think he did it?"

Wingate did not answer right away. After a few seconds he said, "I think he could have."

Spencer gave a couple of slow nods but waited for the other man to go on.

"I heard from George Farrow himself, just about a week ago, that some of these bigger cattlemen might have contracted with Wolf Carlton to take care of what they call the 'rustler problem.'"

Spencer felt a twinge of discomfort. "I've heard of that before."

"It's a term they use in the Association, to avoid calling something by its real name."

"Anderson went on about the Association. Do you think they're behind it?"

Wingate shook his head. "If someone is doing something here, they're doing it on their own initiative. Same as elsewhere. They go through people they know, line up someone like Carlton, and make a contract with him. All spoken, of course— nothing written."

"Naturally." Spencer gave a slight nod.

"Then if they need support, they can get other members to stand behind them."

"Like playing with a stacked deck."

"Sure it is."

Spencer moved his head back and forth in slow motion. "You put it that way, and there doesn't seem to be much a little man can do."

Wingate's brown eyes had a fire behind them. "When you've had a bullet put through you, there's not a damn thing you can do. But that doesn't mean everyone else should turn and run." He paused and looked at his wife, who had come out of the kitchen with a plate of cookies and stood at the corner of the table.

Spencer wasn't sure, but the two seemed to be exchanging some kind of unspoken message, and he did not want to be seen as eavesdropping. He was absentmindedly gazing at the blue pattern that ran around the edge of the plate when he realized Wingate was waiting for him to look up and hear the rest. He gave Wingate his attention.

"The little man's got to stick up for himself, and he's got to stick up for the others like him. When something like this happens, he can't crawl in a hole." Wingate's eyes still blazed.

Spencer gave a brief nod.

"They keep their hands clean. They bring in someone who's good at it. But you just can't let 'em get away with it."

Wingate looked straight at Spencer and then at his wife. She nodded in agreement and turned her eyes to Spencer, who met her full gaze and answered as she had, without words.

Chapter Two

Spencer held his left hand on the dark horse's shoulder as he dragged the currycomb along the ridge of its back. The horse's coat was warmed by the sun, and the animal stood calm with its eyes half closed. Of the three horses in his string that had spent the winter out on the range, this one felt the steadiest beneath Spencer's hand. But he was not fooled. He remembered the horse from the year before, and he knew he needed to be ready when he put his foot in the stirrup and swung his leg over.

Perkins and Trask, the other new cowhand, each had a whole string of seven to go through, so Spencer kept an eye out to see if they needed a hand at any point.

The kid Perkins, in spite of his tendency to ask more questions than some people cared for, was no stranger to ranch work. He had an easy way about him as he worked with the horses, and he didn't seem to mind any job that came his way. As he walked by leading a long-legged sorrel, he paused to look at the horse Spencer was brushing.

"Is he a good 'un?"

"He's all right when he settles down to work."

Perkins had a faint smile as he tipped his head up half an inch to look at the dark horse. He was a slender kid, who looked as if he might put on more muscle and weight as time went on. He had a narrow face, clean-shaven, with a broad area above his upper lip, and his brown eyes were wide open, as if everything in the world was new and pleasant to look at. Even his denim coat and his brown hat with the tall, dented crown and wide brim looked like something he would grow into.

"Every one of 'em's different," he said.

"How do you like that one there?"

The kid ran the back of his fingers across the flat side of his horse's neck. "Pretty good, so far. I like 'em all till they try to do somethin' with me. I'll know more when I put a saddle on 'im."

Spencer took a full glance at the rusty-colored horse. "I think the fella that rode him last year had to get his attention a couple of times."

"I wouldn't be surprised." Perkins gave a light tug on the rope and led the sorrel away.

As Spencer moved around the rump of the dark horse to brush the other side, he caught a glance of Orin Trask. The man had lifted the front left leg of a speckled white horse and was scraping the underside of the hoof. His brown hat, full mustache, dark stubble, and black neckerchief made a contrast against the white body of the animal.

Trask was a quiet type so far, who kept to himself. From the little he said, it became known that his brother had died a year or so earlier. Something like that could turn a fellow quiet and cautious.

He dropped the hoof and stood straight up, so that his mustache and the upturned brim of his hat showed in profile. He was not very tall, maybe medium height or a little shorter, and he had a compact build. In his movements he seemed deliberate, almost wary. Now he made a slow turn of the head, his dark eyes taking in the scene until they rested on Spencer, who gave a light toss of the head. Trask made a small motion in return, then ran his left hand up to the ribs of the horse and moved toward the hind leg.

Loner, but it set well on him.

Spencer went back to currying the dark horse. It was all in a day's work, whether a man was combing out tangles, trimming hooves, or cinching the saddle on a horse for the first time that season. How a man did it was up to him, and if he did it poorly, or did it wrong, the consequences were his. And even if he did things right, he could take a spill that left him lame for life or put him in an early grave. Spencer wondered if something like that had happened to Trask's brother.

A shout from across the yard made the dark horse jump. Spencer, pushing against the horse's flank, looked across its back to see what was going on.

"Hold that son of a bitch!" It was Waltman's voice. The man stood back from a small commotion between two other men and a horse. Waltman was wearing his high-crowned hat, a grayish tan affair that rose straight up with no dents or creases, like a large, round bullet head. He had his hands on his hips as he barked again, "Hold him, damn it!"

The two hired men were pulling down on a rope at the same time they were being jerked up by a brown horse that was rearing back and fighting his head to one side and another. A small cloud of dust was rising, and a pair of stovepipe boots rose out of the dust and sank back into it. That was Galloway. The other man, Kern, in addition to losing his grip on the rope, had lost his hat.

Spencer recognized the setup right away. Waltman liked to lord it over Galloway and Kern, and that was why the big man stood back and let the other two get tossed around. Spencer preferred not to get in the middle of the other men's affairs, but it looked as if these two could use a hand at the moment. Spencer made a quick, smooth move around the hind end of the dark horse, set the currycomb on the ground where it wouldn't be stepped on, and hurried over. He could see now that the horse had a saddle on it, not cinched very tight, and it had slipped to the side.

"Need a hand?" he called as he passed Waltman.

"Yeah, go ahead." The larger man stood with his hands on his hips and his head raised.

Spencer grabbed the dancing tail of the rope, then moved his hands up and pulled back. Galloway in the black boots settled to earth, and Kern of the smelly gray shirt got hold of the rope again, bent at the knees, and sagged his butt like a kid pulling on a church bell.

The horse yanked again, then lost its footing and fell on its left side with a rattling of buckles and a shaking of saddle leather.

"Pull! Pull!" hollered Waltman.

All three men pulled back together, but the horse raised its head, got its front feet underneath it, and rose. Spencer thought it might try to bolt, but instead the animal planted its four feet and shook. The saddle still hung halfway off the left side, smeared with fresh manure, but it did not slip any lower.

"Hold him there," said Waltman. Then turning his head, he called, "Hey, you. Trask. Come over here."

Trask came at a quick walk, his chaps rumpling.

"Go pull the saddle off that horse while these three hold it."

Trask's eyes, beadylike, held on Waltman for a few seconds. "Don't you want to tie him up?"

"Just go get the saddle off."

"I'd tie him up first."

"Tie him up afterwards. Just go—"

Trask cut him short. "You're not the foreman here. Why don't you go reach under him and try to find the latigo?"

"Why, you son of a—"

"I'll get it." It was the kid Perkins, calm but not slow as he walked up to the horse. He patted the animal's neck, ran his left hand down to the shoulder, still patting as he crouched, and reached his right hand under the horse's chest. The horse jumped sideways and settled against the pressure of the rope, and the kid moved forward. He reached again, worked his hand back and forth, then caught the saddle and slid it off, cinches trailing. The blanket fell in the dirt, and Trask, who had been two steps behind Perkins, moved around him and picked it up.

"Tie him up now," said Waltman, "and see about gettin' some hobbles on him." Then he turned to Trask and said, "I don't know what you were afraid of."

Trask fixed his dark eyes on Waltman. "I wasn't afraid. Don't think I was. I just don't jump to and take orders from someone who thinks he's the boss and isn't, especially when there's a better way of doin' things."

Five of the six hired hands sat in chairs along the sunny side of the bunkhouse. The day's work was done, and Mac the cook had not yet rung the triangle. From across the yard, Kern came shuffling on foot, carrying two buckets of water he had dipped from the horse trough.

Waltman kept his eye on the man until he had emptied both buckets into the ridged earthen bowl around a spindly elm seedling not four feet tall. "That's got it, Si," he said.

Kern set the two empty buckets inside the bunkhouse and stood in front of the doorstep at Waltman's left. Slouched with his head tipped, he faced into the sun as it slipped beyond the corrals in the southwest.

He was a nondescript man, of average height with light brown hair and an aquiline nose. He wore no vest, only the gray wool shirt that he never changed. His hat was dust-colored, an oddlooking piece with a low, rounded crown and a rolled brim that made a kind of funnel in front, something like the three-cornered hats of a hundred years earlier. Spencer thought it might be a normal backwoodsman's hat, as Kern came from West Virginia and spoke a kind of coonskin English. Right now he pulled the front of his hat brim down to shade his eyes, then brought out a plug of tobacco and his jackknife. With the plug in his teeth, he moved the blade of his knife up and around, then down between the first knuckle of his left hand and the tip of his nose. For as many times as he had seen the maneuver, Spencer still marveled at the dexterity of a man who was slovenly in so many other ways.

Waltman sat with his chair tipped against the wall of the building. He had his chin tucked into his chest as he gazed down at the bulgy cigarette he was building. After he licked the seam and lit his smoke, he brushed away most of the tobacco grains he had spilled onto his vest. "You'd wonder that some of these horses are gelded," he said. "The way they act up."

"Cut too late," said Kern. "Like a boar hawg." He had been holding his open knife at his side, and now he clicked it shut and put it away.

Waltman took another drag. "Not a one of 'em can't be rode, though. Just a matter of who's got what it takes."

Galloway, who sat tipped back in similar fashion on Waltman's right and pulled smoke from a narrow cigarette, said, "I don't like that big brown bastard. I'd like to see you get on him."

Waltman shrugged off the comment. "I've got my own horses to ride."

"Well, whether it's me or someone else, a man can get hurt on that one."

"If he looks that bad, there's no reason to pass him off on someone else. If it comes to it, we can talk to Al about that one. We might cull him."

"Be fine with me." Galloway hiked his right boot onto his knee, while he kept the heel of his left boot hooked in the rung of his chair. He was a short, thin man, and with his trousers tucked into his boots, plus his black, narrow vest of matching leather, and his short black hat with its narrow brim, he looked as if he might be in some kind of uniform. That illusion was enhanced by the way he wore his pistol—on the left side, butt forward, in cross-draw position, as if it were a stubby descendant of a saber.

The boots and the pistol reminded Spencer of pictures of Napoleon, though the resemblance stopped there. Galloway had straight, coarse brown hair and, though he was thin as a snipe, his brown eyes were set far apart. He rolled and smoked tight cigarettes, and the veins stood up on the backs of his hands. Napoleon, as Spencer recalled, was built more like a partridge and wore white gloves.

No one spoke for a few minutes. Galloway finished his cigarette, pinched it out, and dropped the butt. Waltman had burned his cigarette down close to his fingertips and was setting his chair on all fours when the sound of horse hooves came from the left. Galloway set his chair down and craned his neck forward. Spencer, with his view blocked, decided he could wait ten seconds to see who was riding into the yard.

Waltman stood up and stepped forward as the horse came in at a walk. Galloway rose as well, and with quick swipes of the hand he brushed off the front of his clothes. Waltman, whose hat had been cocked off center when he was propped against the wall, reset it so that it sat straight up.

The head of a horse moved into Spencer's view—a cream-colored palomino with a milky blaze. Then came the reins and neck, and the rider himself, who drew the horse to a stop in front of Waltman.

Spencer recognized the man right away as Cliff Ardmore, a friend and fellow rancher of Al Jerome. He was wearing a dark blue coat with matching vest and wool pants, topped with a flat-crowned hat of the same color. As usual, he was smiling.

"Well, hallo, Dick," he sang out. "Good to see you."

"Good to see you, too, Cliff."

Ardmore swung down and held the horse by one rein. He was wearing deerskin riding gloves, which he did not take off as he shook hands with Waltman. Then, moving around in front of the horse, he caught the other rein and held them both as he shook hands with Kern and Galloway. He gave a smiling nod to each one and said, "Boys," by way of greeting the two of them.

Now Spencer stood up, as did Perkins and Trask at his right. Ardmore handed his reins to Waltman, set his hat back on his head an inch or so, and moved forward. Still with a smile, he gave his hand and said, "Spence."

"Evenin', sir." Spencer noted the high, pale forehead, the rosy complexion, and the bluish eyes not very wide open because of little puffs in the lower lids. His light brown mustache, the same color as his hair, ended at the corners of his mouth, where his cheeks were beginning to chub out.

Ardmore looked past Spencer and said, "A couple of new hands?" As the man stepped past, he brushed back his frock coat and gave a view of his ivory-handled revolver. Then he held out his right hand and said, "Cliff Ardmore. How do you do?"

"Just fine, sir. Millard Perkins. Pleased to meet you."

Ardmore gave an up-and-down glance as he nodded. "Perkins. Pleased to meet you as well." He moved on to Trask, went through the same routine, and walked back to take his reins. As he did, Spencer thought the man might have put on a little weight, as the lower part of his vest was spreading. Maybe he had had an easy winter.

With his reins in hand, Ardmore pivoted on his heel and faced Waltman and the rest of the men from that angle. From his coat pocket he took out a dark cigarillo and transferred it to the hand that held the reins. Next he fished out a match, struck it, and lit the small cigar.

As he blew away the smoke, he raised his head and glanced in the direction of the ranch house. "Couldn't ask for better weather, could we?"

"Sure couldn't," said Waltman.

"Sleep out one night, though, and it's bound to turn off cold and wet." Ardmore smiled as he shifted his stance.

"That's the way it seems to go." Waltman's voice was relaxed but still gravelly.

Ardmore blew another small cloud into the air. "I suppose your boss is at home."

Waltman smiled. "Last I knew."

"Well, I'd better go see him, too." Holding up his cigar between two gloved fingers, he waved and said, "See you later, boys."

The men all answered in like fashion, and Ardmore walked toward the ranch house, leading the palomino with his left hand and trailing smoke over his right shoulder.

Waltman raised his head in Kern's direction. "Si," he began, "why don't you see about supper? Save Mac from having to ring the bell."

Kern dragged his feet into the bunkhouse and came back to the doorway a minute later. "Right away," he said. "Y'all might as well come in."

The men bunched up behind Galloway, who was scraping his boot soles on the doorstep.

Waltman stood to one side, and as Perkins moved next to him, the kid asked, "How do you cull horses here?"

Waltman shrugged. "Like they do in other places. Take 'em down in a draw and shoot 'em."

"They don't just turn 'em loose?"

"Nah. They join up with their old pals in the winter. No good in that. Better to be done with 'em."

After a couple of seconds Perkins said, "That would be too bad for the brown horse, if that was what happened to him."

"Do you want him in your string?"

"Not necessarily."

Waltman patted him on the shoulder. "Don't worry about it, kid. It's one of those things that happen."

Al Jerome came to the supper table after the other men had begun to eat. He took off his hat and hung it on a peg, so that the dark crown with its peak and four dents stuck out into view. He took a seat at the end of the table next to Waltman and across from Kern and Galloway.

"Cliff go home?" asked Waltman.

"Oh, yeah. He's got things to tend to. He just stopped by to go through a few details about round-up." Jerome spoke across the table. "Say, Scot, could you hand me a biscuit? Thanks."

As Galloway held out a tin plate of biscuits, Kern slid the salt shaker in front of the boss's place. Then McCafferty the cook appeared on his right with a plate of fried beef and potatoes.

"Thanks, Mac."

The cook stood back without a word and wiped his hands on his apron. His pink bald head with its fringe of white hair shone in the lamplight. He was a red-faced man with washed-out eyes, a white mustache, and an unfirm chin; and his head tipped forward in conformity with his potbelly and curved shoulders. His eyes followed the boss's movements until Jerome cut off a piece of meat and stuck it in his mouth. Then the cook went back to the kitchen.

"Everything go all right today?" Jerome did not look up as he cut into the meat again.

"No real trouble," said Waltman. "One or two we might have a question about."

Galloway spoke into his plate. "Big brown horse that's got a lot of fight in him."

Jerome reached for the salt. "You've got a few days to take that out of him. Did you get enough to eat, Si?"

"I sure did."

"Well, there's plenty of everything." Jerome raised his chin toward Kern's empty plate.

"I've et enough, thanks."

Mac appeared with a large tin coffeepot and poured a cup for the boss. He set the pot on the wooden tabletop and moved away.

Kern poured himself a cup and handed the pot to Galloway, who passed it to Waltman.

Galloway seemed as if he wanted to say something, but Waltman spoke ahead of him. "Perk's got a good hand with horses."

Jerome cast a glance down the table at the kid and smiled.

Now Galloway spoke. "Maybe he can do more with the brown horse than I can."

"Give it a couple of days," said Jerome. "Kid's new to his string, let him work on that." The boss looked past Spencer and said, "How about you, Trask? Horses all right?"

"No problems with any of mine."

"That's good."

The men ate in silence for a few minutes. Kern got up, put his plate and fork in the wreck pan, and went to the door to spit outside. Galloway folded his knife and put it away, pushed back his chair, and began to roll one of his tight cigarettes. Perk, who never wasted time with his grub, left his plate in the pan and went to his bunk. Trask followed a minute later, and Spencer was about to do the same when the boss spoke.

"Don't leave just yet."

"Oh?" Spencer settled into his seat again.

Waltman pushed back his chair, giving Jerome a clear field of vision, then lowered his eyes. His hand moved toward the vest pocket where he kept his cigarette makings, and then he let the hand fall away.

The boss cut off a strip from the hunk of fried beef, turned it crosswise, and cut it again. Without looking up, he said, "You want to be careful, Spence."

Spencer looked at the boss even though the man did not raise his eyes. "I try to be."

"Oh, I know. Everyone does, or thinks he does."

Spencer frowned. If there had been any trouble, it was between Waltman and Trask. "I think you might have to help me out, sir. I'm not sure what you have in mind."

Jerome looked at him now. "Well, as you know, there's been a little trouble. Not here, but out there." He waved his knife.

"Yes, sir. I knew that."

"And a man's got to be careful who he fraternizes with. You know, that element."

The scene opened in Spencer's mind—the warm house, Collins Wingate, the woman named Eva. Then came a fainter image of the dusty rider Anderson, the tense face and worried eyes. Someone had seen him at one of those moments and had reported it. From the timing, Spencer imagined Ardmore had informed Jerome, but it was hard to guess whether ivory-handled Ardmore had made the observation or had passed it on from someone who did.

"I'm not sure how far a fellow has to go to be fraternizing," he answered.

"I think you probably have an idea. You don't have to invite them into your tavern, serve them free ale, and let your wife and daughters sit in their laps." Jerome gave a light laugh. "You know, like the redcoats in the stories."

Spencer laughed with him. "I remember one or two of those."

"Anyway, I think you know what I mean."

"I believe I do." Spencer glanced aside and saw that Waltman was taking in the whole scene.

"No crime or penalty," the boss continued, lifting another piece of meat with his fork. "Just better, all the way around."

"I understand."

Jerome gave him a direct look. "And how about the horses in your string? Any of them give any trouble?"

"None to speak of. If I get piled by one tomorrow I might change my mind. But it's all part of the work."

"Isn't that the truth? And I know you're doing a good job."

"Thank you, sir." Spencer kept to his chair as Jerome finished his meal, drank his coffee, and handed his plate and cup to Mac.

When the boss had picked his hat off the peg and gone out, Spence made ready to go to his bunk. As he went to move, however, Waltman spoke up.

"Couldn't help overhearin' what Al said."

Galloway, sitting with his long boot hiked up onto his left knee, gave an audible sniff. Spencer glanced at him and back at the man across the table.

"Just some friendly advice," said Waltman, with his tomcat squint.

"Uh-huh."

"If you want to stay on at this ranch and fit in, you need to see how things fall on one side of the line and another." Waltman leaned back, reached into his vest pocket, and now pulled out the cloth sack with the makings.

"I guess I'm beginning to see that."

"And not cause problems by going over the line." The man raised his eyebrows and stared down at the bag he was opening.

Spencer did not say anything. He wondered if the would-be foreman was in confidence with Jerome and Ardmore or if he was just picking up the opportunity to try what he hadn't been able to do with Trask.

"Of course," Waltman went on, shaking tobacco into a troughed paper, "if you don't want to go along and would rather bite the hand that feeds you, that's up to you."

Spencer felt his blood rising. "I'll tell you what I want. I want to decide for myself if it's all right to talk to someone else, regardless of what size of an outfit a man has."

Waltman caught the tag of the string in his teeth and pulled the bag shut. "I didn't say there was anything wrong with it. I was just sayin' what was wise and unwise." He hefted the little bag. "Like I said, just friendly advice."

Chapter Three

Spencer rode into the town of Farlow with Trask on one side and Perkins on the other. They came in from the south and turned left onto the main street. Two blocks west, on the north side, they dismounted and tied their horses in front of the Rawhide Saloon.

Up on the board sidewalk, the other two let Spencer go first. As he pushed through the swinging doors, the place had the same look as always. A bar with a brass foot rail and a dark-stained top ran nearly the length of the back wall. Centered in back of the bar, a mirror about four feet by six feet rose in a heavy frame of two dark posts and a crosspiece. Off toward each end of the bar, at the same height as the mirror, hung a set of deer antlers. Two men stood at the left end of the bar, while the bartender stood at the other end, reading a newspaper by the light of the open side door.

He looked up as the spurred boot heels sounded on the wooden floor. Folding the newspaper, he set it next to the cashbox beneath the mirror and turned to wait on his customers.

Being a tall man, he leaned forward as he kept both hands flat on the bar top. Spencer had seen the barkeep in that posture many times, and he did not think the man held himself that way for support, for he was not heavy. Nor did he present his hands as a grocer would, showing a readiness to weigh a scoop of beans or to wrap a chunk of bacon. Rather, he seemed to put his hands there with the light touch of a habitual cardplayer, who kept both hands on the table to keep from causing uneasiness in others.

A few paces from the bar, Spencer called, "Good afternoon, Rex."

"Hello, boys." The man was almost expressionless as he gazed through eyeglasses, and the slight inclination of his head made his thin mouth and disappearing chin less visible than usual.

"Let's set 'em up," said Spencer. "Bottle and three glasses." Trask and then Perkins took their places at his left.

Rex straightened up, slid his hands from the bar, and tended to the order. He set three small glasses in front of the men, filled each one with whiskey, and set the bottle aside.

Spencer pushed a silver dollar toward him. "First round's mine."

Rex took the coin, rang the cashbox, and set two coins on the bar top. Leaving the bottle where it stood, he went to the end of the bar where the other two patrons stood.

"Here's to it," said Spencer, raising his glass.

Trask and Perkins raised theirs. Each man took a sip and set his glass on the bar.

Perkins, who stood farthest on the left, said, "Don't want to drink all that at once."

"Some do," said Trask. "Toss it off with a wink."

Perkins motioned with his wide brim. "No, I meant the whole bottle."

"Some men do that, too. Maybe not in a gulp, but in short order. You'll see it."

"Oh, I have." After a few seconds, Perkins added, "Old Mac, he looks like a good one for that."

"Don't know," said Trask.

"Oh, well, neither do I. Just a thought."

Spencer leaned froward and turned to speak. "Tell us, Perk. Do you have a girl back in Ohio?"

"I thought I did. But soon as I left, someone else walked in. Just as well, I guess."

Trask stepped back a pace, and Spencer saw the kid staring at his glass.

"Sorry I asked."

"No, it's all right. There's plenty more." The kid's face brightened. "Just a matter of findin' 'em."

"That's right," said Spencer. "You can have some fun yet. You know what they say. Once a fella gets married and settles down, that's the end of punchin' cows." He turned to Trask. "Isn't that right?"

"That's what they say."

"No more followin' the wagon," Spencer continued, "much less comin' into places like this."

"That wouldn't be all bad," said Perkins. "I figger when I settle down, I'd like to get my own place and run a few horses. That's the part of cowpunchin' I like the best anyway." He tipped his head, as if in reflection of what he had just said. "Of course, who wouldn't?"

"Hard to say," said Trask. "Some don't seem to care for any of it, and they still do it."

"Like Kern?"

"I wasn't thinkin' of anyone in particular. Then there's others, they seem to like managin' property, even if it's not theirs." Trask turned to Spencer. "Isn't that right?"

"Oh, yeah. They act like every cow and calf is theirs. Jealouslike."

Perkins came back into the conversation. "Me, I could never care if there was a hundred more or a hundred less."

"Neither could I," Trask said, "but that interest runs pretty strong with some men, owners and punchers both."

Strong enough to kill for, Spencer thought. But instead of saying it, he put his fist on the bar and declared, "I'd say Perk's got it right. Girls and horses, count cows when you have to."

The kid tucked his chin, lowered his voice, and said, "Damn betcha." It was good for a short laugh with all three.

Time passed in light talk for a while longer. Trask ordered the next round, and as Rex was pouring the drinks, a motion at the side door shut out some of the daylight for a second. As the man came into the saloon, Spencer saw that it was Cliff Ardmore.

The man sauntered to the end of the bar and gazed at the deer antlers until Rex came and took his order.

Spencer looked aside. For a moment he thought Ardmore was trying not to notice the A-J riders, but as he turned to catch another glimpse, he saw Ardmore's face widen in recognition.

The man took out a dark cigarillo and lit it. Then he picked up the glass that had just been set before him, and after taking a drink he came around the end of the bar and approached the group of three riders. He was dressed as before, and he swept his coat back long enough to show the ivory handle of his six-gun.

Smiling, he called out, "Hallo, boys."

Spencer and the other two returned the greeting. "Out for a last howl before the roundup starts?"

"Something like that," said Spencer. He gave the man a casual once-over, but he couldn't get a sense of whether Ardmore had given the report to Jerome, and if he had, whether it tinged his thoughts at the moment.

"Good for you. Where's the rest of the boys?" Though Ardmore raised his brows, the puffs still showed beneath his eyes, and his cheeks were not lank.

"I think they were comin' along a ways behind us," said Spencer. "They might be in town already. I believe they favor the Horseshoe."

Ardmore smiled again. "Each man to his own." Raising his cigarillo and tossing a light glance at Perkins, he added, "I think there's girls there, later on in the evening."

"They come in here, too," said Spencer.

"Oh, I wouldn't know. It's just what I've heard tell." Ardmore raised his eyebrows and turned down his mouth, in an exaggeration of innocence. He took a drink and transferred the glass to the hand that held the little cigar.

"Same here," Spencer replied. "I'm always home by sundown."

"I should be, too." Ardmore patted Spencer on the shoulder, then took in all three. "Well, boys, I just stopped in for a quick one. I suppose I'll see you all again before long." He tossed down the rest of his drink and set the empty glass on the bar. After giving a wave of his free hand and calling out "So long" to Rex, he left through the side door. He became a dark shape and then a shadow before the daylight came through again.

"A little goodwill," observed Trask.

"You think he went to the Horseshoe?" asked Perkins.

Spencer couldn't help smiling. "Just for a quick one."

The talk went on. Perkins bought a round, and then Spencer bought another. The light area at the side door turned gray and went to darkness. Rex lit two lamps above the bar. A few other men drifted in, but no one crowded. Perkins and Spencer were each turned sideways to the bar, looking inward on their group of three. Perkins told the story of how his father had been killed in a railway accident and how his mother had married a storekeeper in Canton.

At the close of that story, which ended with his coming out West, he seemed to be wavering on his feet. After a short silence among the three, Perkins moved his eyes toward Trask and said, "You've never told us how your brother died."

"It's not a good one to talk about."

"Neither is mine, I guess. Lost my pa, lost my girl. Spencer must be thinkin', this kid feels sorry for himself."

"Not really," said Spencer. "Everyone's got some sorrow, some more than others, and most people's stories are interestin'. If I had one, I'd tell it."

The kid's eyelids were drooping as he turned to Trask again. "I'm sorry. I didn't mean to be pryin'."

"It's not pryin'. There's nothin' private or secret about it, it's just somethin' that's got nothin' good to it. But now that you got me started, I'll go ahead and tell it. And there's not much to it."

"Well, I didn't—"

Trask held up his hand. "Just let me tell it." He took a sip of whiskey and said, "It happened a little over a year ago, right after that whole boil-over where they killed the two men at the K. C. Ranch. Only this was down on the other side of the Medicine Bow Mountains, and nobody made any connections. I don't think there was, either, except with all that other hubbub, this got treated like a local incident. Which it was, in a way." He took another sip. "Here's how it went. My brother had his own little place, ran a few head and worked for wages when he could. Of course, these big operators don't like that, a man havin' his own cattle and workin' for someone else."

"They think he's gonna rustle from 'em," said Perkins.

"That's the theory. Whether he does or not, they mark him for a rustler. Then his name gets on a list, and he comes out his cabin door one mornin' and he catches a bullet."

"And that's how it happened to him?"

Trask nodded. "It was hired out, and no one could trace it."

Spencer had a tight feeling in his stomach. It was like Wingate had told it. "No idea, then," he said. "They bring someone in from a long ways off, and he goes back to where he came from."

"A place to stay, between jobs, and look respectable. Maybe he's got a wife and daughter some place, somethin' like that, but if he does, they don't know what kind of a son of a bitch he is. Then before long, he goes off on his next job."

Perkins spoke up. "Do you have an idea who it was, then?"

"Not the slightest. Just speakin' in general."

"It's sure as hell a bad deal," said the kid. "Call someone a rustler, when half the people in this country, from what I've heard, have branded a slick calf or two."

Trask's eyes flickered in Spencer's direction and back to Perkins. "Don't know a thing about that, either."

Spencer held his tongue. He thought he should say something, but there was no reason to talk about a few winter calves that got branded well before these two hands came to the ranch. As for the future, he supposed he was outside Al Jerome's circle of confidence and wouldn't be offered that kind of work even if he wanted it.

He was sorting through his thoughts when a loud voice came up behind Perkins. The kid flinched as a large hand clapped him on the shoulder, and his hat tumbled off behind him.

The voice boomed. "Where's the bitch, you old houn' dog?"

Perkins had bewilderment on his face as he was pulled halfway around. He tipped his head back and frowned.

A tall, bearded man with jug ears and a battered hat raised his brows in surprise. "Oh, I thought you was Brewster."

Perkins scowled. "Do I look like him?"

"Not now." The man raised his head, smiling with his mouth open and showing his Adam's apple.

"Well, I don't like my hat being knocked off." Perk's voice had a bit of a slur to it.

"Ah, I didn't mean it."

"I don't care. I don't like it."

"Don't get flustered, kid."

"I don't like someone knockin' off my hat."

Spencer could tell that Perk was in a state of mind in which repetition made good sense.

The jug-eared man's face spread open in a sarcastic smile. "Oh, you're a real cowboy, aren't you? Texas style?"

"Here," said Trask, stepping between them. "There's no need for any of this." He bent over, picked up the young man's hat, and handed it to him. Then he turned to the tall man. "That's probably enough."

"Are you a cowboy too?" The man's face still had a taunt to it as he looked down on the shorter individual.

Trask's eyes went hard and beady. "It doesn't matter."

The expression on the man's face sagged, and he turned and walked away.

As Perkins settled his hat onto his head, he grumbled, "I don't care if he didn't mean it. He could have admitted he made a mistake."

"Forget it," said Trask.

"He's right," Spencer added. "Some people just won't admit when they're wrong. Forget about him. Think about somethin' better, like girls."

Perkins smiled. "Shall we go to the Horseshoe?"

"Company's no better there," said Spencer. "There might be some girls in here in a little while."

Trask resumed standing where he had been before. "Do you know who that fella is?"

Spencer glanced in the tall man's direction. "I think he's a mule skinner. I wouldn't expect anything more from him."

"Neither would I." Trask looked to each side. "You know, this is the only saloon I can think of where just about everyone's got his back to the front door."

"I think you're right. Usually they have the bar along one of the side walls, especially when it's not a big place. But the room's not deep enough here. They'd have to knock out that back wall. This must have been somethin' else before it was a saloon."

Trask shrugged. "Shouldn't matter."

"Stand around to one side."

A little laugh came up. "And turn my back to the mule skinner, let him come up on me?"

"Here, change places with me."

"No, no."

"Let's take a table. Perk, you want to sit down?"

"Fine with me."

"There's only two," said Trask, "and one's taken. What if someone wants to play cards?"

"Evenin', Spencer."

The voice at his left caused Spencer to turn. In a sweep he recognized the dust-pale hat with up-turned brim, the drooping blond mustache, and the tense face. "Evenin', Anderson. Do you know these boys?"

After the introductions, the little group fell silent. Background voices rose and fell; tobacco smoke hung in the lamplight. Anderson stood with his thumbs hooked in his pockets.

"Buy you a drink?" Spencer offered.

Anderson raised his head as if he needed to think about it. "Sure," he said. "And thanks."

Spencer signaled to Rex, and a minute later he handed the drink to Anderson.

"Thanks again."

"Don't mention it."

The dusty rider settled back on his heels as if he were relaxed, but his hand was tense on the glass, and his bloodshot eyes were restless.

"Still at the ranch?" Spencer asked.

The man gave a tight nod, took a drink, and said, "I wish I could clear out. I've got to wait to get paid, though."

"Has anything else happened?"

"No, nothin'. Me 'n' the other boys, we try to act like everything's normal, but every time you step outside, you wonder if it's the end."

Spencer took a casual glance at the man. "Did you come into town alone? Where are the other two?"

Anderson looked downward and lowered his voice. "They're at a meeting. I didn't want to go, so they left me off here. Said they'd pick me up on the way back."

"Is the meeting here in town?"

"Yeah, at the barbershop. Wingate called it."

Spencer felt a sinking sensation. He would just as soon not know it.

Trask motioned with his head. "Do you think that's what brought him out?"

Making a quarter turn to follow Trask's gesture, Spencer saw a man standing next to the spot where Ardmore had stood earlier. It was Wolf Carlton, and he did not yet have a drink in front of him, so Spencer figured the man had just come in the side door.

Carlton had his gaze fixed on something behind the bar and below the level of the mirror, so Spencer got a look at him. He was not wearing the fur coat he had worn each time Spencer had seen him during the winter. Rather, he wore a jacket of dark gray wool and a hat of similar color. The top piece had a single crease along the crown, and it looked as if it had not seen much hard wear.

Carlton raised his head as Rex approached with a bottle and glass. In the lamplight his features were visible—the head tapering from a round cranium to a narrow set of jaws and chin; large, round eyes and prominent cheekbones; and a trimmed, yellowish brown mustache that seemed to grow out of his nostrils.

"You know him?" Spencer asked, turning back.

Trask spoke in a low, casual tone. "Know of him."

"Jesus," said Anderson, his voice quavering. "Why did he have to come in?" The worried man shifted position so that Spencer stood between him and the stock detective.

"Just doin' his work," said Trask.

Carlton stood gazing straight ahead, in the uneven posture of a man who had one foot on the rail. Although he did not look around, Spencer assumed he had gotten a view of who was in the saloon.

With his right hand on the bar, Carlton rotated his drink glass. Then he picked it up and downed the whole drink at once. Setting the glass down, he stepped back from the bar and came around the end.

Anderson shifted again to keep his back to the man, but Spencer stayed where he was. As Carlton came into view, Spencer saw that the man had a lean build, leaner than he had appeared previously in the fur coat. With a quick upward scan, Spencer noted the narrow, peaked ears and the hair growing out of the nostrils. Then the man was past, only to pause and shift on his feet. The tip of his holster showed below the hem of his jacket. Spencer observed the narrow-fitting lace-up boots with no spurs, and then Carlton walked to the front door and out into the night.

"Don't worry," said Spencer. "He's gone."

"I don't like him," Anderson rasped.

"Neither do I." Spencer tightened his shoulders. Carlton's passing that close had given him a bit of a chill as well, but he wasn't going to say anything about it. Then, seeing that Anderson's glass was empty, he said, "Do you want another drink?"

"Nah. Well, all right. I'll owe you one."

"Think nothin' of it."

A while later, Anderson's two fellow riders came in for him. Neither of them seemed interested in staying, so Anderson finished his drink, thanked Spencer again, and left with his pards.

"Nervous sort," said Trask.

"Those three all rode for George Farrow."

"I gathered that. I don't blame him for being scared, but he's kinda small-fry, I'd think—him and his pals. Hard to tell him that, though."

"I'd say." Spencer looked at Perkins, who leaned with his left forearm on the bar. "What do you say, Perk? Are you keepin' your eyes open for the girls?"

Perkins straightened up and took in a breath. "I don't think there's gonna be any. Not even to look at."

"We can leave after this drink if you want."

"Fine with me." Perk's voice sounded tired, and his frame settled as he leaned on the bar again.

Spencer turned to Trask, who nodded.

From down the bar, a loud voice rose above the others.

> *I don't know, but I've been told,*
> *There's honeypots that's made of gold—*

Spencer shifted to keep track of who was standing in back of him, and as he turned to face Perkins and Trask, a man came in the front door. He wore a gray wool suit and vest, with a white shirt and a Windsor tie. His hat was something in the style of Carlton's, with a lengthwise crease, but it curled up on the sides and had a dull ribbon for a hatband. Spencer recognized him from his clothes and from his bronzed complexion and green eyes. The man went to the end of the bar and took the place where Ardmore had stood earlier, not far from the antlers.

"Who's that?" came Trask's voice, low.

"He's a lawyer. Name's Warren Robinson."

"Do you think he was at the meeting?"

"Not the one Anderson mentioned," replied Spencer. "I don't know of any others."

The lawyer stood calm and relaxed as Rex the bartender pulled out an odd-shaped green bottle and poured liquor into a wide glass. Robinson pushed a coin across the bar and raised his glass for a sniff.

"He drinks Scotch whiskey," said Spencer. "They keep it for him."

"His privilege. Perk, you still awake?"

The kid's eyes were half closed as he raised his head and smiled. "You bet."

The voice from down the bar rang out again.

> *I don't know, but I've been told,*
> *The girls up north are awful cold—*

Spencer set his empty glass on the bar. "I'm ready," he said. As he turned to walk away, he almost bumped into Collins Wingate.

The man was clean-shaven and dressed for town, with a brown coat and vest and a starched white shirt with a collar. His hat was set back a ways, and his eyes were clear.

"How do you do, Spencer?"

"Just fine. Yourself?"

"Good enough. Buy you a drink?"

"No, thanks. We've been in here long enough. By the way, these are a couple of punchers I work with. Orin Trask, Perk Perkins."

"Collins Wingate."

After the men shook hands all around, Spencer said, "We stayed up late with Perk to see if any feathers and lace came through."

"It's not that late, actually," said Wingate, raising his chin and casting a glance each way down the bar. "Seems there's a lot of fellas out, though."

Spencer let his eyes meet Wingate's. "They've come and gone. Cliff Ardmore was in for a little while earlier, and then Fred Carlton came through."

"I see."

"Is there someone you're lookin' for?"

"No, not really. I just thought I'd drop in and see who's here." Wingate's eyes went from Perkins and Trask back to Spencer. "If you fellows are going out to the ranch, I could ride with you for a ways. If you don't mind."

"Not at all," said Spencer. "You boys?"

Trask shrugged. "Fine with me."

"Me, too," said Perkins. "Just don't knock my hat off."

Wingate smiled at the kid. "I wouldn't do something like that. I can barely hang on to my own." Then he seemed to catch a glimpse of Robinson the lawyer for the first time. He gave a light wave, which the man in the gray suit returned. "Friend," he said.

Spencer nodded, and he and Wingate followed Trask and Perkins out of the Rawhide Saloon.

Chapter Four

The sky showed pink in the east when Spencer stepped out of the bunkhouse. The ranch yard lay still and quiet. Although he had lived and worked in this part of the country for nearly ten years, he was still impressed with the quietness of a ranch such as Al Jerome's. In other places, earlier in life, he had heard roosters crowing well before daylight. In some, he had become accustomed to the quacking of ducks, the hissing honk of geese, and the queer cheep of guinea hens. In one place, which he often recalled on mornings such as this, he would hear the long cry of peacocks and see them perched like sentries on the peak of the calving shed, dark forms in early daylight, their long tails lying on the roof and reaching almost to the eaves. By contrast, the A-J seemed empty. It had no calves bawling, no milk cow mooing, not even a dog to bark. Other ranches such as this one had dogs, but many of them were like the A-J and had only men and horses.

As Spencer crossed the yard and approached the corrals, he could hear movement—horses shifting their feet, pushing against one another. A snuffle, a nicker. They knew someone was coming.

He went into the barn for his rope, found it by touch more than by sight, and came back out into the morning light. At the corral gate he picked out the dun, then opened the gate and closed it behind him. The dun knew it was his turn, but he wanted to play the game. Bunched between two other horses, he kept to the far edge of the corral. Spencer followed, shaking out a loop. The horse on the dun's left, a gray with a short mane, broke away. Spencer let him go, cut off the dun so it couldn't turn the corner, and then threw the loop when the horse tried to switch back. Once the dun knew it was over, he fell into place and followed Spencer to the gate.

Perkins and Trask were coming out of the bunkhouse as Spencer led the horse to the hitching rail. He imagined Galloway and Waltman were having a second cigarette, and Kern wasn't going to move until he had to. It was all the same to Spencer. He took satisfaction in knowing that he was doing his work and minding his own business.

Spencer tied the horse with a single-bow slipknot, then went to the rope-handled box for a brush and currycomb. As he started brushing, he saw Perkins and Trask come out of the barn with their ropes. He heard the kid's voice but did not try to pick up the words. The dun stood gentle beneath Spencer's hand, the warmth emanating in the cool of morning, the soft hair lifting after each pass of the brush.

The sky turned yellow as the sun began to show behind the hills in the east. Spencer moved around the hind end of the horse and brushed the off side. Changing the brush for the steel currycomb, he used the long teeth on the back of the tool to comb the horse's mane and tail. The dun had shed early, and Spencer had been riding him every two or three days, so with the brushing and combing, the horse's coat was smooth, and the mane and tail had few tangles.

Al Jerome's voice sounded from behind. "Go ahead and put a saddle on him, Spence. I've got an errand for you."

Spencer looked over his shoulder, where the boss stood with the sun rising at his back. He must have left the table ahead of Waltman, Kern, and Galloway, as those three were just crossing the yard toward the barn.

Spencer peered at the shadowed face. "I'll take him over there to saddle him, then. I suppose I'll get to the others when I come back—dependin' on how long the job takes, of course."

"It shouldn't take long." The boss reached inside his coat and drew out an envelope. "I'd like you to deliver this to Cliff Ardmore." He held it forward.

Spencer moved three steps and took the letter. He was glad to see it was sealed. Transferring it to his left hand, he tucked it into his jacket pocket, where it was held firm by his gloves. "Should be easy enough," he said. Then, on reflection, he added, "What if he's not there?"

"Oh, someone will be. You can give it to his wife."

"Good enough." Spencer motioned toward the dun. "Well, I guess I'll get going."

Jerome's voice held him. "I would have sent Dick, and I don't think he would have minded, but I thought he should stay to help out these other fellas. They say they've got a couple of horses that are strong-headed. You're pretty well caught up on yours, aren't you?"

"Oh, yeah, and like I said, I'll get to the others when I come back."

"Well, don't take long, anyway."

"I won't." Spencer moved to the horse and pulled the knot loose as Jerome walked back to the bunkhouse.

It took less than ten minutes to get the saddle and bridle on, so the sun had not yet risen very high when Spencer rode north out of the ranch. From time to time he held the reins in his right hand and used his left to make sure the letter was still snug in his pocket.

Three miles out, he rode past the trail that led west to Wingate's place. Even though he told himself it was better to know nothing, he couldn't dismiss his curiosity about what had gone on in the meeting at the barbershop. On the ride out from town the night before, Wingate had not said a word about it. He had bid a pleasant good night and ridden off toward his own place, where Spencer could now imagine smoke rising from the stovepipe and sunlight shining on the little house and stable.

As he rode on, his thought returned to one detail of his earlier conversation with Al Jerome. It struck him as unusual, in a small way, that the boss would take the trouble to explain why he was sending Spencer instead of Waltman. As a general practice, Jerome gave orders and didn't bother to give reasons unless a question came up.

It made Spencer wonder if he was being tested—if, for example, he was being given a clear opportunity to drop by Wingate's and share some knowledge.

Jerome might even have arranged to have someone on the lookout. It would be hard for the boss to know that Spencer had had more than enough opportunity to confab with Wingate the night before and had brushed it off, so if he was setting up a test, it was a waste of effort and a rather amusing one to Spencer.

On he rode a couple more miles as the trail curved northeast through a gap in the buttes. Out on the other side, he took the trail east toward Ardmore's place. The sun had risen enough that it did not shine straight into Spencer's eyes, but he pulled his hat brim down an inch and enjoyed the warmth of the sunshine on his face.

The range spread out ahead of him in rolling grassland, where new grass showed dark beneath the withered curls from last year. Three miles ahead, Ardmore's would lie to the north. South of that would be Farrow's. Spencer imagined Anderson and the other two punchers huddled around the stove, wondering what their next move would be. Well, he wasn't going to go there, either. He would deliver this message and get back to the A-J before noon dinner.

As he came to the trail that led north into Ardmore's place, he thought he saw something to the southeast. It looked like a rider who poked his head above a hill and turned back. Spencer shrugged. It was none of his matter. He turned north and felt the sun on his right as he rode on, noting again the condition of the range and appreciating that it had not been overgrazed.

Over the last rise and into the ranch yard, he did not see any movement except a couple of horses looking out over the top rail of the corral. The place was soundless. Spencer wondered what time Ardmore had gotten in the night before and whether he was up and about yet.

He felt in his pocket yet one more time to be sure of the letter, then turned the dun toward a hitching post in front of the house. Swinging down, he drew the loose reins together and tied them to the iron ring.

After two knocks on the door and the sound of the latch, he expected to see Ardmore appear puffy-eyed and maybe a bit pasty. But when the door opened, he was met by a woman with dark blue eyes, fair skin, and wavy blonde hair.

"What is it?" she asked, her eyes moving over him.

"Mrs. Ardmore?"

"Yes." She made a small frown.

He thought she might have taken him for one of her husband's newly hired men. "My name's Spencer Prescott," he said. "I work for Al Jerome. He sent me over here with a letter for your husband. Is he home?"

"Come on in," she said, moving aside and opening the door.

He took off his hat as he stepped into the front room. From the corner of his eye he saw her close the door behind him; not wanting to seem curious, he stood looking at the legs of a fabric-covered chair. He expected to hear footsteps from within, but only the woman's motion sounded as she moved around and faced him.

"I can take it," she said, without raising her hands from her side.

"Oh." He shifted his hat to his right hand, drew out the letter, and held it toward her. He felt it slide from his fingers as she took it.

"You've come a long ways," she said. "Would you like some coffee?"

"I suppose it would be all right. Is Mr. Ardmore around?"

She turned and set the letter on a sideboard. "Not right now," she said. Facing him again, she showed her small, white, even teeth. "He's gone to town."

"Oh, I see." Spencer glanced around the room, not wanting to look straight at her for too long. He settled on the curtained window. "I didn't see any of his men around."

"They're out gathering horses."

"Don't they have them in already?"

"He says they're missing some, so he sent them out again." She moved toward a doorway off to his right. "Here, have a seat. I'll get some coffee."

As she turned, she straightened her shoulders, and he could not help noticing her pert bosom. Nor could he ignore her rounded hips as she moved away with her full-length dress swishing.

He felt dry in the mouth, but he went to the straight-backed chair she had indicated, and he sat with his hat in both hands.

She came out of the kitchen with two cups of coffee on saucers. "Here," she said, setting them down. "Do you take sugar?"

"No, thank you."

She smoothed her dress on her hips and sat across the corner of the table. "What did you say your name is?"

"Spencer Prescott, ma'am."

Her pretty teeth showed in her smile. "You can call me ma'am if you wish, but my name's Julia."

"Well, I'm pleased to meet you." He raised his cup and leaned to sip from it.

"And likewise." She did not touch her coffee but put her hands together beneath her bosom. "How long have you been with Al Jerome?"

"A couple of years."

"Then you know some of the others."

He shrugged. "In passing."

"Tell me this if you can, then," she began, her dark blue eyes sparkling. "Why do men have to go to town so much?"

Spencer recalled Ardmore and his manner of spreading goodwill. Then he imagined the man keeping a lookout to see if Spencer was visiting Wingate. If he was out there, it might be more amusing than Spencer imagined earlier. "I don't know," he said, taking a drink of coffee. "Business, I suppose."

"He goes to Cheyenne in the winter, he goes out on the range during roundup, and in between times he goes to town."

"Busy man, I guess."

He saw the tip of her tongue, then her teeth again as she said, "You don't get around that much, do you?"

"I'm too busy," he said, feeling a little tremor as he laughed. "Or I should say, the boss keeps me busy at my own work."

She had a placid expression, as if she were waiting for him to say more.

He brushed a glance her way. "Keeps me out of trouble, as the saying goes."

"Oh," she said, turning her head in a teasing look. "What kind of trouble could you get into?"

The nervous laugh came up in him again. "I don't know. I've never been there."

She shifted in her chair, and her hands moved in her lap. "That's good," she said. "People who stay out of trouble are either well behaved or very careful."

He gave a light shrug, as if to seem indifferent, but he could feel a stirring. "A person could be both," he said.

"Oh, yes. Careful, no matter what. You seem like you're very careful."

"I try to be." He felt again a dryness in his mouth, and he moistened his lips.

"Not the type to throw caution to the wind at the first opportunity."

He could still feel the excitement, but he steadied himself. "Oh, no. Think twice, look twice, before you go ahead."

"Look twice, then go ahead? That's very good." She gave her teasing look again.

Now the temptation was rising again, but he knew he had his back to the door, and her husband could walk in at any time. "Well, it *is* funny when you put it that way, but for the present I think I'm going to look once and think twice."

Her blue eyes softened, and her parted lips were tender. "That's very gallant of you. I'll remember it."

He smiled. "No harm in that." He drank his coffee down to less than half the little cup. Rising from his chair, he said, "I'm sure you understand that I need to be getting back."

"Of course." She rose to face him, and she held out her hand. "It's been a pleasure to visit with you."

"The pleasure is mine." He took her warm hand and released it, and he wondered if she felt a tremor in his.

"And if you have occasion to come by again—"

"I'll be as charmed as I am now." Tipping his head toward the table, he said, "Thank you for the coffee."

"You're quite welcome. I hope to see you again."

"So do I." As she opened the door for him, he appreciated her profile once more and then walked out into the sunlight. He did not look back as he untied the horse, led him into the yard, and swung aboard.

On his way out he passed what looked like a bunkhouse on his left. It had seemed lifeless on the way in, but now a man in an apron stood slouched in the doorway. He had dark, thinning hair combed in shiny streaks across the top of his head. His brown eyes followed Spencer, and when the horse and rider were even with the door, the man lifted a cigarette to his mouth and turned to the side to blow away the smoke.

A hundred yards farther, then up and over a rise, Spencer let out a long breath of relief. He had no doubt that he could have had an adventure with Mrs. Ardmore, but he was glad he had resisted the temptation. As for some moment in the future—some second look—that was a rosy idea.

The image of her wavy blonde hair, her sparkling blue eyes, her pretty teeth and delicate lips, as well as her other charms, stayed with him on the ride back to the ranch. It had been a rousing moment or two. When he got to the bunkhouse, the others had already eaten, so he ate by himself and carried on a little further with his daydreaming. Then he went out to resume his day's work.

Back in the company of the other men at the A-J, Spencer began to think that dallying with any woman in Julia Ardmore's circumstances would be worse than unwise. It might seem bold at the time, just as he had felt bold when he was in her presence and enclosed by four walls. But to take the idea out in the open and turn it this way and that, a man could see the danger and the folly.

To begin with, men got shot for tricks like that, at least in this part of the country where few men had wives and all men had guns. And if a man didn't get shot, he could count on getting shunned. Here were Waltman, Galloway, and Kern, not to mention Mac the cook, who would side automatically with Ardmore on behalf of his friend, their boss. Even Trask and Perkins would have reason to keep their distance. It was not a good prospect for a man who wanted to mind his own business.

Spencer set down the hoof he had been scraping, and he rose to straighten his back. Perkins was riding the long-legged sorrel in the round corral, and Trask was saddling the gray horse with the short mane. On the other side of the yard, closer to the barn, Waltman stood under his bullet-head hat and watched as Kern and Galloway worked with the big brown horse. They had it tied close to a snubbing post, blindfolded with a denim jacket, and hobbled front and back.

Galloway was smoothing out the blanket on the horse's back, and Kern stood by with the saddle.

This time they managed to get the saddle on and cinched down tight. For the next two hours, the brown horse stood bound and blinded with the saddle in place. No one climbed on or even stepped into the stirrup. In midafternoon, Kern came out of the barn, footing slow under the weight of a hundred-pound sack of grain. Waltman helped him heave the burden up onto the seat of the saddle, where they tied it across with a manila rope. Again they left the horse on its own, this time under the deadweight.

Toward the end of the day, as Spencer came back into the yard after taking the dark horse out for a ride, he saw a horseman leaving the ranch and heading north. The dark horse had bolted a couple of times, so Spencer was paying close attention and staying ready for any surprise. He didn't recognize the rider at that distance, and he figured there were others like him, going from one ranch to another as the outfits got ready for roundup.

What he saw next put the other rider out of his mind. Waltman was holding the gate open to the round corral, while Galloway, with Kern at his side, was leading the tall brown horse into the corral. Waltman, erect in his high-crowned hat, had the bearing of a stockade guard. Galloway looked over his shoulder every couple of steps, while Kern shuffled along in his usual way.

Spencer dismounted, took off the bridle, and tied the dark horse with the neck rope. Hanging the bridle and reins on the saddle horn, he loosened the front cinch.

Waltman was closing the gate, and Perkins was climbing onto the corral rails. Trask was walking toward the scene of action, so Spencer decided he would watch as well.

The round corral was nearly six feet high, and the rails did not have gaps between them, just cracks here and there. The best way to get a view was to climb up, so Spencer grabbed a hold and pulled himself up to sit with Perkins and Trask, like three rail birds.

From where he sat, Spencer could see that Galloway and company had gotten a bridle onto the brown horse but had left the rope around its neck. Waltman on one side and Kern on the other held the horse by the bit while Galloway coiled the rope and tied it on the saddle string next to the swells. Then Galloway rubbed his hands together, drew on a pair of leather gloves, and reached up for the saddle horn. Giving a push and a boost with his right foot, he stabbed the toe of his left boot into the stirrup and swung aboard. His left hand closed tight on to the reins.

Bunched and ready in his black hat, black vest, white shirt, and long black boots, Galloway looked like a magpie on the back of the big horse. The short-brimmed black hat jerked up and down to signal that the rider was ready. Waltman and Kern each let go, and the horse leaped forward. It plunged about five yards, braced its front legs, and kicked up in back, causing Kern to swing his hand at the flying dirt and to back up to the fence. Then the horse went up on all fours, left the ground, came down with a jolt, and bucked again. Galloway's hat tumbled away. As the horse cut to its left, swapped ends, and continued bucking, the sound of heaving and grunting mixed with the rustle and creak of the rigging. Galloway rose from the saddle with his right leg swinging loose, came down again, and then with a pop went sailing. The horse kept bucking for a couple more jumps and came to a stop on the other side of the corral. The scene became still for a moment as the dust settled.

Waltman, who had moved back toward the gate, came forward to help Galloway up out of the dirt. Kern brought him his hat, and at a word from Waltman, he moved in slow steps toward the horse. Meanwhile Galloway stood up, tested his right leg, and went limping toward the gate. Kern got a hold of the reins and followed his pal.

"Show's over," said Trask.

Perkins smiled as he swiveled on the rail, swung his legs, and bailed off. As the other two climbed down, he said, "That's a lot of horse."

"Got a hankerin' to ride him?" asked Spencer.

"Not today," said the kid.

For supper, Mac served up a pot of beans with floating chunks of bacon rind, plus the expected tin plates of biscuits. Al Jerome came to the bunkhouse after everyone else had gotten under way. He hung his hat on its peg, with the peak of the crown and its four dents sticking forward. He took his seat at the end of the table, facing the door, and did not speak to anyone except Waltman on his left. Spencer thought the boss looked perturbed about something, and before the meal was over, the reason became evident.

"Boys," he said, "I got a complaint today." He held his spoon straight up in his fist. "You know, Cliff Ardmore sent a man over here."

"Crow," said Waltman. Then, after a sharp look from Jerome, he added, "Crow. That's his name."

"Well, it's not his name I want to talk about. It's about the message his boss sent."

All the hired men had stopped eating, and they all looked at Jerome.

"He says, Ardmore does, that he doesn't want any of my men coming into his house when he's not there."

Waltman, Galloway, and Kern all turned to glare at Spencer, and even Mac the cook raised his washed-out eyes and stared. Trask and Perkins were off to the edge of Spencer's vision, but he imagined they were taking in plenty as well.

With so many eyes on him, Spencer struggled to come up with words that made sense. "I didn't know he wasn't there, sir."

Jerome gave an impatient frown. "Didn't know?"

"No, I didn't. I knocked on the door, and his wife—"

"We don't mention her."

"Of course." Spencer cleared his throat. "To put it another way, then, I knocked on the door, and when it was opened, I asked if he was at home. I don't believe I was told that he was or wasn't, but I was invited in, and so I thought he was."

"But he wasn't, of course."

"No. I found that out right afterwards, so I handed over your letter."

"But you didn't leave right away."

"No, it was a minute or two, maybe longer."

"How long?" Jerome snapped.

Spencer recalled the man in the bunkhouse door, who might well have had the minutes counted. "Long enough to drink half a cup of coffee. A small cup."

"Did you think it was your place to do that?"

"I must have forgotten my place for a moment, sir. But I assure you, nothing happened."

Jerome glared. "Nothing happened? You went into the man's house. I assure you that's something. If it weren't, I wouldn't have gotten a letter from him later the same day."

Spencer nodded and cast his eyes down at the table. "It was a mistake," he said. "It was my fault. I was into it before I realized it, and I could have gotten out a few minutes sooner. Should have."

"Call it a blunder, call it a blockhead thing to do, but I'm telling this to all of you at once." Jerome set down his spoon and looked around, summoning the men with his authority.

Now that he was not the center of attention for a moment, Spencer had an awareness that the boss could have handled the problem in a different way but chose to stage it like this.

"There's no room for anyone getting out of line," Jerome went on. "I've said it before. Everyone's got to stick together, work together. That means in this outfit as well as with other outfits. Take someone like Cliff Ardmore—we're in all of this together. Our two outfits and a couple others do this whole roundup, follow the same wagon, and eat the same chuck. We can't have any grudges or suspicions, big or small, hangin' in the air. So I'm sayin', you see somethin' or hear somethin', you don't be part of it. And if you say somethin', don't worry about someone callin' you a stool pigeon." After a second's pause he added, "These are not easy times. We've got some serious work ahead of us. There's no need to get stuck in the past, so let's just move ahead."

Jerome finished his meal without speaking again. He handed his bowl and spoon to Mac, said good night to all, and left the table. At the doorway he paused to settle his hat onto his head, and then he opened the door and went out.

Silence prevailed at the table. Perkins and Task went to their bunks, and Kern brought in firewood for the morning. Galloway and Waltman rolled their respective cigarettes and sat smoking.

Spencer waited, but no one spoke. He expected Waltman to pick up where the boss left off, but the tomcat smoked on and exchanged an occasional glance with Galloway, who shifted now and then and gave a visible wince.

Spencer got up and went to his own bunk. From where he lay, he had a clear view of Waltman sitting beneath the haze of tobacco smoke. Waltman the company man. Spencer wondered. Suppose Waltman had been the one to take the letter, and the missus had invited him in for a cup of coffee. Spencer liked to think she had more refined tastes in men, but there was no telling, and if it were all in sport, she might take a fancy to a larger man. Suppose he had gone inside and had a conversation similar to the one Spencer had had. It was hard to imagine Waltman being too noble to go that far. To the contrary, it was easy to imagine him thinking that he and he only could bring out that spark, and it was easy to imagine him seeing how far it could go. But put him on the outside, and let him know of someone who had been on the inside, or seemed to, and he gave it the silent, superior treatment.

That was all right, too. It was no worse than his friendly advice, and in some ways it was no different.

Chapter Five

Spencer awoke to the sound of low voices. The lamp above the mess table had been lit, and he heard the usual muffled sounds of Mac rummaging in the kitchen. No one sat at the table, so the voices came from the area where the men slept. Raising his head, Spencer saw Waltman's shadowed form standing by Galloway's bunk. Words were passing back and forth, and the tone sounded matter-of-fact and not conspiratorial.

Spencer rolled out of his bunk and got dressed in the half-light. By the time he arrived at the table, three of the hired men were sitting there. Kern sat across from Waltman, and Trask had a seat a couple of places farther down from Kern. No one seemed inclined to speak, so Spencer sat down between Kern and Trask to join the mute group. Kern handed him a cup from the stack and then slid him the coffeepot.

The door opened, and Al Jerome came in. He hung his hat on the peg and took his seat next to Waltman, who signaled for the coffeepot. When the boss had poured himself a cup, Waltman spoke.

"Scot says he feels all bunged-up this morning, too stiff and sore to get out of bed. I told him to get up anyway, see what you have to say."

Jerome pushed out his lips and blew steam from his coffee. "I hope he's not hurt too bad."

"Kinda short order to find someone else."

"Well, it's not just that," said the boss.

A minute later, Galloway came hobbling and grimacing into the lamplight. He passed behind Jerome and around the end of the table, letting out short, openmouthed breaths. At his chair he turned like a crippled man, leaned his hand on the table, and lowered himself with a groan.

"Don't feel worth a damn," he said.

"I can see that." Jerome's eyes went up and down. "Why don't you take it easy today, get up and move around when you can, so you don't get any stiffer?"

"I think that would be the best." Galloway took a quick sniff and leaned forward to pour himself a cup of coffee.

Perkins came to the table and sat not far from Waltman's left. He had shaved the night before, and his face looked smooth and youthful.

Waltman turned to him and smiled. "Perk, what do you think of ridin' the brown horse? Scot doesn't feel up to anything like that today."

The kid's eyes went to Galloway, who sat looking mournful with his arms across his chest. "Sure. I can give it a try."

"Sounds fine," said the boss. "Dick and Si can give you a hand." He cast an empty glance toward Spencer and Trask. "The rest of you are all right with your own work, I'm sure."

They both nodded.

Mac appeared with a platter of hotcakes. He stooped to set it on the end of the table and went for another. He handed it to Waltman, who held it across the table to Kern. Each man served himself, and as Perkins handed the plate to Trask, Waltman turned his large head and said, "Eat up, kid. You're gonna need it."

For his first task of the day, Spencer went to work on a lightweight sorrel that he considered to be the last horse in his string. As he brushed and combed the animal and then undertook to trim its hooves, he kept an eye out over his shoulder to see if anything broke loose in the group Waltman was supervising.

They snubbed the brown horse as they did the day before, then put on the blindfold, hobbles, and saddle. The only difference was that they did not use Galloway's rigging. Perkins did not have his own saddle, so he used one belonging to the ranch, and he cinched it onto the fractious horse. When he was done, Waltman sent Kern for the sack of grain, and the three of them tied it on. They left the horse standing, and each of them went on to his own work.

A couple of hours into the morning, a wind began to pick up out of the southeast. That was the way it was in late spring, Spencer reflected. The wind could blow from one direction, then change and blow from another. It was an annoyance when a man was trying to lay on a saddle blanket, and it made skittish horses hard to mount. He was glad he wasn't the one to have to ride the brown horse today.

In the latter part of the morning when the horse had been standing at the snubbing post for about three hours, Waltman called to Kern and Perkins. Spencer, now working on the buckskin from his string, kept an eye on things again.

First they unloaded the grain sack, and as Kern was toting it back to the barn, Perkins leaned down and took off the hobbles. Next he untied the blindfold and pulled it away, and Waltman handed him the bridle. The kid slipped it on, settling the bit in place and buckling the latch. He handed the reins to Kern, who had come back and was standing by.

All this time, Waltman stood with his hands on his hips. "Go ahead and untie him," he called.

Perkins nodded, tipped his wide-brimmed hat against the wind, and picked at the knot. After a minute he got the rope untied, then coiled it and tied it to the saddle. As he turned away, he held his hat with one hand and said, "I'm gonna go trade this for somethin' else, so it won't fly off and spook him."

"All right," said Waltman. "We'll be over by the corral."

The kid went to the bunkhouse as Kern led the horse and followed Waltman. Spencer patted the buckskin on the shoulder and began to walk toward the round corral. Trask fell in beside him without saying anything.

Kern had stopped a few yards from the gate and stood, slouching, as Waltman slid the wooden latch and stepped backward to swing the gate out. As the big man changed his angle, the wind caught his hat, lifted it clear, and tumbled it forward.

The brown horse pulled back, raising his front feet off the ground as he pulled the reins free. He cut to the left in midair and came down facing west, with the wind at his tail. By the time Kern had collected himself from jumping aside, the horse was on a full gallop with the reins trailing out on the left.

Waltman went running after his hat, stooped, rose, ran again, and caught up with it. As he came back brushing it off, he barked at Kern, "Close the gate, damn it. Hell of a lot of good it's doin' now."

Kern dragged his feet as he pulled the gate behind him. At the post he turned around, came outside, and slid the latch.

Waltman scowled as he turned his hat over and inspected it. "Some of us is goin' to have to go after that horse. I'll see what Al says." Holding his hat by his side, he walked to the ranch house.

Spencer and Trask headed back to their work and met Perkins, who had come from the bunkhouse and was wearing a knit wool cap with a little beak. When they told him what happened, he said, "Well, who knows if anyone's gonna ride that horse today?"

Waltman came out of the ranch house, pressing down on his hat and leaning into the wind. "Spencer," he called out, "Al said for you and Trask to go with me. Perk, you can go back to whatever you were doin' before."

Perkins twisted his mouth to one side and looked at Waltman's hat. Without a word he pivoted on his heel and walked away.

Trask's voice came out. "That horse might be hard to catch."

"We'll get him," said Waltman, "if only for the outfit that's on him." He stalked off toward the bunkhouse.

Spencer went about saddling the buckskin while Trask brought out the speckled white horse and got him ready. Waltman came out of the bunkhouse wearing a stocking cap that made his head look like a large, dark burr. He was carrying a leather scabbard with a rifle butt sticking out.

Spencer and Trask waited as Waltman saddled a deep-chested sorrel and strapped on the scabbard. The big man led the horse into the middle of the yard, turned out the stirrup, stepped into it, and swung aboard. The other two mounted up as well, and Spencer waved so long to Perkins as the horses moved out onto the trail.

"He'll be runnin' with his ass to the wind," said Waltman, "and he'll slow down after a little bit." He hit a lope to the northwest, and the other two followed.

A mile and a half out, Waltman slowed his horse to a walk and pointed at the ground. "Looks like he went this way."

Spencer studied the marks in the dirt and then the surroundings. The three horsemen had stopped at the mouth of a draw that narrowed and became steeper as it turned to the west. Spencer reined his horse aside and let Waltman take the lead again.

Around the curve and three hundred yards ahead, the draw ended in a header with an eroded overhang and no loose horse in view. Waltman pushed his horse up the left side, and the other two followed. Up on top, Waltman brought his horse to a halt and said, "There he is, the son of a bitch."

The brown horse, still saddled and with the reins trailing, stood in profile looking at them from about two hundred yards away. He broke into a trot and angled away.

For the next half hour, there followed a cat-and-mouse game. The horse would run two or three hundred yards at a time—now north, now west, now to the northwest—and each time would stop and stare until the pursuers came up again. But they never got closer than they did the first time.

"Let's fan out," said Waltman. "Try to get him that way."

Spencer and Trask looked at each other but did as they were told. As either of them could have predicted, however, the horse cut through the empty space between any two riders he pleased. All three men had their ropes ready, but none of them got a chance to throw a loop. After about twenty minutes of forming triangles and regrouping, Waltman signaled to the other two and trotted forward to meet them.

"This isn't working," he said. "Let's try it the other way, just followin' him, and see if he gets tired of the game."

They fell into place again, with Waltman leading and the other two a few steps behind on each side.

After another fifteen minutes of stop-and-go, Waltman reined his horse in and said, "I've had just about enough of this." He swung down from the saddle and said, "Here, one of you hold my horse."

Spencer and Trask both dismounted, and Trask took Waltman's reins. With his back turned, the big man in the knitted cap looked like a ruffian from the loading docks, until he pulled the lever-action rifle from the scabbard and swung it up and around to get clear of the horses. With his hardened face in view, he looked once again like Waltman the bully.

He moved to the left, where the ground rose in a little knoll. He settled into a prone position, propped himself up by the elbows, and adjusted his hips to get the rifle aimed.

Spencer clamped on the reins and looked over his shoulder to keep an eye on the brown horse. He heard the snickety-click of the lever action. Then the rifle crashed, sending a loud, piercing wave of sound rolling over the grassland. The buckskin tried to jump back, but Spencer held on.

The brown horse fell on its rear and twisted sideways as it fought with its front legs to get up. Its mouth was open in a scream. The lever action clicked again, and a second rifle blast ripped the air. A puff of dirt jumped up beyond the brown horse's withers.

Spencer hung on to the reins, grabbed the buckskin by the headstall, and kept the horse under control.

"Damn," said Waltman. He jacked in another shell, and the ejected brass casing landed on the curled grass. This time the man seemed to be bearing down, for he did not fire right away. The wounded horse pawed at the dirt, and its screaming carried across the distance. The rifle crashed again, the horse snapped over, and the sound of a bullet hitting a solid object came back on the air.

The whole scene went quiet. The buckskin settled down, as did the two horses Trask was holding. Spencer's mouth was dry, and his stomach had taken a jolt. He hoped no one was within miles to have heard any of this, and he dreaded the idea of anyone seeing him take part in such an act. He brought his eyes around to Trask, whose expression matched the way Spencer felt.

Waltman had pushed himself up from the ground. "Hell of a way to have to do it," he said. He turned the rifle over and slid it into the scabbard, trigger guard up. "I guess we'd better go get the gear off of it."

The three men walked leading their horses. Spencer did not want to look at the brown horse, but he knew he was going to have to. He kept his eyes on the ground, and before long the hooves and the large belly came into view.

"Of all the luck," said Waltman as the men came to a stop. "Cut the headstall with that last shot."

After several minutes of tugging, first on the saddle and then on the hocks of the dead horse, the men got the saddle free.

Waltman stood back and surveyed the wreckage. "Three pieces," he said. "Let's do it this way. Trask, you take the bridle and reins. Spencer, you take the blanket, and I'll take the saddle."

Spencer picked up the blanket, a long, heavy one that had been folded twice to make a triple thickness. He tied it onto the back of his saddle, where he would have to swing his leg high to go over it.

First, though, he and Trask had to hand the saddle up to Waltman where he was seated. "This is awkward as hell," said the big man, "but I guess I'll have to make do." He took the fifty-pound saddle by the horn and rested it on his right thigh. Looking at the scene for a last time, he said, "I suppose that's it."

He reined his horse around and started in the direction of the A-J. Spencer and Trask mounted up and fell in as before. The wind had died down at some point that Spencer hadn't noticed, so he didn't have to hold his head into the wind now. Up ahead, Waltman in the dark knitted cap looked like a hulking lumberjack holding a huge dead turkey by the neck.

The group rode southeast, following more of a straight path than they had taken in pursuit of the horse. The country was much the same, with dips and rises and an occasional draw. Off to the south twenty miles ran a line of bluffs, chalky in the noonday sun, and far to the southeast, well beyond the ranch headquarters, rose one of the few hills big enough to be called a mountain in this rolling grassland. Even it would be a foothill in the mountains to the west, but out on the plains it distinguished itself, and from this direction it served as a landmark for riding toward the A-J.

After traveling about two miles, the men came over a low hill to a swale where a horse stood alone in the bottom. At first it reminded Spencer of the horse from earlier in the day, as it had a saddle on its back and a set of reins hanging to the ground; but it was a smaller mount, a sorrel with white stockings in front.

Waltman brought his horse to a stop. "I'd like to borrow that horse to carry this saddle for me," he said.

Spencer peered at the horse, trying to make out what seemed familiar about it. "I don't know. If he's out here wanderin' around, he might have thrown some rider who'd like to get him back."

The three men moved forward, and as they did, an object on the ground came into view on the other side of the sorrel. Spencer made out the white sleeve of a shirt, the brown of a vest, and the dark length of a pair of legs in trousers.

He turned to Trask. "That looks like the horse Wingate was ridin' the other evenin', doesn't it?"

Trask's mouth shifted before he spoke. "It does."

"We'd better take a look," said Spencer. "If his horse threw him, he might be hurt bad." Even as he said it, though, he felt a tenseness moving through his upper body. A horse that had thrown a rider would probably not come back and stand that close. If a man fell off, with or without help, the horse might.

Closer, he saw that the man did not move, would never move again. Wingate lay on his face with his left arm alongside his body and his right arm outstretched. A few yards away, his hat lay on the grass. A low breeze riffled the man's hair, the midday sun shone on the dull white sleeves of his work shirt, and a dark spot showed on the vest, a couple of inches off center to the right.

Spencer shook his head. "We went past here, maybe half a mile to the north, a little over an hour ago."

"It would have been too late even then," said Trask. "That stain is pretty dark."

Spencer dismounted and knelt by the body. He touched the arm, which had gone cold and stiff. "I'd say this could have happened last night, yesterday afternoon."

Waltman, who had lagged behind, came to the scene at a walk, his horse's hooves swishing through the grass. "It's him, huh?"

"Yes, it is." Spencer stood up and scanned the area around him. "Looks like someone came up behind him."

Wingate's horse had moved away at the approach of the men, and now Trask followed him on horseback and caught the reins. Spencer waited for him to come back.

"It looks like it's up to us," he said. "Not that I want to, but we can't just leave him here. His place is north of here two, maybe three miles, and a ways east."

Waltman cleared his throat. "I'm good and tired of this son of a bitch already," he said. "Here, hold it for me."

Spencer took the saddle and set it on the ground. "We'll need his horse to take him in on, of course."

"I know," said Waltman. "And I've got to get that saddle back, one way or the other. I just wanted to rest my arm for a minute."

Spencer turned to the north. "It won't take all three of us to take him home. You and I can do it, can't we, Orin?"

"Sure," said Trask. He nudged his horse and led the sorrel around to the other side of the body, where he dismounted.

"Need help loadin' him?" Waltman's voice did not sound very eager.

"Nah, that's all right." Spencer looked at the body, the horse, and the sky to the north, above the rim of the depression they were in. "The whole thing'll take us a while. We'll need to go to his place, then to town to report it, then back to the ranch. Don't expect us till after dark."

Waltman moved his head side to side. "Why don't you take him straight to town?"

"I think his wife should know first."

"Well, you're doin' it. I s'pose you can give me that saddle again. Over here on this side." He reined his horse around as Spencer picked up the saddle and hoisted it to him. "Thanks," he said. "I'll tell Al what's goin' on." With a change of voice he uttered, "Hep," and the horse moved away at a fast walk.

Spencer decided to ride into the Wingate place from the west side so Trask could wait by the stable, out of view, while Spencer delivered the news. It would not have been a bad plan, except that no one answered the door. He walked all around the house, calling out, but he got no response. He tried both doors and found them locked, which he didn't mind. The idea of going into the house, or even opening a door and calling, did not appeal to him.

Leading his horse out to the middle of the yard, he waved to Trask. Horse and rider came forward, leading the other horse and burden.

Spencer's eyes met Trask's and then traveled to the body. "It looks as if we take him to town after all. I can't find anyone at home."

"Do you think she went lookin' for him, or went to town?"

"No tellin'." Spencer glanced up at the sun, which had passed the high point. "I think we should take him in. We could lose a lot of time lookin' for her, especially if she's not out there."

Trask gazed away to the south, then tipped his head in the direction of town. "I guess we'd better get goin', then."

***

The deputy came out onto the board sidewalk as Spencer and Trask were tying the horses at the hitching rail. He was a portly man with a full head of graying hair and a couple of days' worth of stubble that brought out his jowls. The star on his shirt was the only clean thing about him, as his shirt and trousers were sagging and wrinkled, and his suspenders had old sweat stains.

"Sheriff's not here," he announced. "Won't be back till later." He pushed out his lower lip, brought it back, and said, "If that's who I think it is, his wife's been in to report him missin'. She's over at the Paragon, waitin' for the sheriff to come back."

Spencer looked in the direction of the hotel and returned to the deputy. "No one's been out to look for him, then?"

"I've had to mind the office, 'pecifically for things like this."

"Well, I suppose we should give you an account of where we found the body, but in the meanwhile I don't think we should leave him out in the street, or bring her out to see him like this."

"Natcherly. I think you can bring 'im around to the back of the barbershop, and they'll take him there."

Trask spoke up. "I can do that."

Spencer glanced toward the hotel again. "Good enough. If I get done here before you come back, I'll be over there."

"All right." Trask untied the sorrel and turned to lead it away.

"Come on in and give me the details," said the deputy. "It shouldn't take long."

Ten minutes later, when Spencer stepped back out onto the sidewalk, he could tell the news had spread. Two men sitting on a bench across the street, their upper bodies in the shade of the butcher shop awning, were staring at him. A third man had just left them and was headed across the street at an angle toward the Horse-shoe Saloon.

Spencer turned left, putting all three men out of view, and walked toward the hotel. From the moment he had decided to deliver the news himself, he had been trying to form the right words, but they still had not come. In a couple more minutes, he was going to have to say something.

Boot heels sounded on the boards behind him. Fast steps, then a voice calling his name. "Spencer! Spencer!"

He turned to see the dust-pale hat, blond mustache, and haggard face of Kent Anderson. The man stopped within a foot of Spencer, and in an agitated voice that he was trying to keep to a low whisper, he said, "Is it true? Did they kill Wingate?"

Spencer drew his head back from the smell of whiskey. "Someone did."

"Jesus," said Anderson in his raspy voice. "This is worse than ever."

"It's not good, that's for sure."

Anderson's eyes blazed. "Not good? My God, man, they're killing us one by one. And you just stand there and say it's not good."

"Look," said Spencer, working hard to hold his temper. "I found him. I brought him in. And I'm on my way to tell his wife. Don't tell me I'm just standing here."

"All right, all right. I just—" The man's voice choked off, and he looked away. He brushed his eyes and turned back to face Spencer. "All right," he said again, heaving a deep breath. "I've stayed here this long just to get my wages. I finally got paid this morning, and I was going to leave tomorrow. But I'm not waiting. I'm pullin' out today."

"I can't blame you. This place is poison."

Anderson's words came in a rush. "I'm clearin' out. No one can blame me. You know that, you just said it. I can't just wait and let 'em get me, too. I'd be crazy." His eyes darted from side to side, and he lowered his voice. "I'm goin' to southern Utah, a long ways from here. My brother can help me get work. I don't care if I have to tend sheep or get calluses from a pitchfork. I'm a cowhand, and not a bad one, but I'm done with this country."

Spencer looked at the man, who seemed to have slipped a peg. "I wish you the best of luck."

"Thanks, Spence, and you, too." Anderson put out his hand, gave a push-pull handshake, and stood planted as Spencer turned and went on his way.

The tightness came back to his chest and abdomen, spread through his shoulders. He could feel his hands unsteady. He went down into the street, across, back up. At the middle of the block he came to the hotel entrance, a door set in on his left.

As he walked in, he saw a woman sitting in an upholstered chair a ways back from the light that came in from the window. A dark woman in a dark gray dress. Her eyes stayed on him as she stood up and came forward into the better light.

"Mrs. Wingate, I'm sorry to be the one to tell you this, but—"

Her blue eyes were wet, and she held a handkerchief to her cheek. "I've already been told. A few minutes ago."

His spirit sank. "I'm sorry."

"I know. You were his friend." She dabbed at her other cheek, sobbed, and wiped her eyes. Her dark hair, which at some point had been tied up in a coil, had wisps and strands coming loose. "I'm sorry I don't have more fortitude," she said. "I've been up all night, sick with worry, and then this."

"I wish there was something I could do."

Her blue eyes met his. "Is there nothing?"

"I don't know."

She lowered her head as she shook it. "Collins told me something like this could happen. Especially after what happened to George Farrow." She raised her eyes, still moist. "He tried to get some of the other small ranchers to pull together, say they'd stick up for one another, but none of them wanted to go along. After that he told me it left him out on the ice alone. Worse off than before."

"He might have been right," said Spencer in a quiet tone.

Her voice came quick. "You heard him before. He knew what these big cattlemen were up to. Call a man a rustler, and have him taken care of. If someone asks why, that's the reason that goes around."

Spencer felt small, insignificant, as he said, "I know."

Her eyes held him now. "He was not a rustler. You know that."

"Yes, I know."

"He was honest. You were his friend, and you knew that." Her eyes searched Spencer. "I hope you can do something."

He hesitated. "I'm not sure what more I can do. I was the one, along with a couple of other riders, who found him. Two of us brought him in, and I gave the report to the sheriff's deputy. I told him I didn't think anyone had a fair reason to do this."

"Is that all—all you can do?" Her voice was halting, but it had a note of impatience.

He winced. "I don't know. I can't take it into my own hands, you know. I can't track down the killer and bring him in on a rope." He lowered his voice. "I'll tell you what I can do, though. I can keep my eyes and ears open, which I've been doing all along, and I can help you in whatever way I can."

Her brows tightened. "And how is that?"

"For the moment, I can give you some advice."

Her face seemed to fall.

"I know it's not much, but I'm not in any position to do more. I might be later on, but for the time being I would recommend that you hire a man to look out for your interests. It's called a rep. He represents you at the roundup. By law and by custom, he's got a right to be there. I'd guess that whoever did this was hoping that your place and Farrow's would fall apart and be easy pickin's."

Her eyes were clear as she said, "Can you be my rep?"

The question gave him a pang, but he overcame it. "I don't think I would last very long, and then I'd be no good to anyone. But if I can stick out the season where I am—"

"I understand," she said, her voice firm now.

"I don't know if you do. I was your husband's friend, and I'll be yours. But I can't do it if I step in front of a train."

"It's all right. I was hoping for a quick answer, but I'll try to follow your advice. It's just that things have happened so quick to me—"

"I'm sorry for it, Mrs. Wingate. Please believe me."

"I do, and I thank you. And now if you'll excuse me, I think I need to sort through what I have to do in the next few days."

"If there's anything—"

"It's quite all right from here." She took a deep breath and said, in a steady voice, "We'll see how time treats us."

When Spencer walked out into the daylight, Trask was waiting with his speckled white horse and Spencer's buckskin. The sight of the tri-fold blanket tied onto the back of his own saddle reminded Spencer of the roundabout trail that had gotten them to this point in the day. The sun was ready to slip in the west, and a long ride to the ranch lay ahead of them.

It was indeed a long ride, through late afternoon, dusk, and nightfall. All along the way, Spencer carried an image of Eva Wingate, the woman who asked if he could do something. Inadequate though he felt for not being able to offer more, he thought he was right in what he said, that being careful might help him be able to do more later on. Being careful—that was Jerome's watchword, reinforced by Waltman's friendly advice. They didn't mean it in the way he was undertaking it, which was all the more reason for him to keep his eyes and ears open. Eva Wingate didn't think he meant to do much by that, but he hoped to show her he could.

Chapter Six

Ardmore's wagon joined Al Jerome's for the first ten days of roundup. Starting at a point just east of the A-J, the crew combed the range in a broad sweep northeast and then north. Ardmore and Jerome were in frequent company, as they kept a count on the herd at each gather point and on all the calves the men branded. They took their shifts at day-herding, ate with the men at meals, and slept on the ground like the rest of the crew.

In the middle of those ten days when the outfit was closest to Ardmore's headquarters, he rode home in the evening and showed up again in the morning. At the end of the ten days, Ardmore's wagon went on its way to the east as Jerome's went north. One of Ardmore's men stayed with the A-J as rep, while a man Jerome hired out of Cheyenne went on to rep with Ardmore's crew. As Spencer understood it, Jerome's man had been repping at another roundup and would move on to yet another crew when he was done with Ardmore.

Throughout the ten-day interval, Spencer was impressed by how little recognition was given to recent events. Warren Robinson, the lawyer who was administering George Farrow's estate, hired a man to rep for the deceased rancher, whose three hired hands had all gone off to other places. As the cows and calves passed through the gather, men would call out "Farrow," just as they used his name freely in all references to the other stock of his that they counted or to his ranch when they were near it. Through all of those comments, Spencer did not hear a single reference to the man's death or to the reason his men decamped. Farrow might just as well have been an absentee owner, distant in time as well as place, as his name itself sounded when it was called out above the bawling of calves and the lowing of the herd.

Spencer also noted that no hint or reference was made to his having crossed the threshold of Ardmore's house. Jerome had mentioned it but once, that evening in the bunkhouse, and had said they were not going to dwell on things in the past. During roundup, Ardmore also acted as if what was in the past could stay there. He moved with ease among all the men, calling them by name and patting them on the shoulder. On the surface he treated Spencer no different from any of the others, as if nothing had ever happened.

In Spencer's view, that was the way with both of these cattlemen, in matters large and small. Their actions seemed to say, if we don't talk about it, if we don't recognize it, it didn't happen. The situation reminded Spencer of scenes he had witnessed and stories he had heard about children who had been humiliated and then, in view of the rest of the family, had been treated as if nothing irregular had gone on. There was an illusion of pardon, almost a reward for having taken the chastisement, along with the pretense that nothing had taken place to begin with.

When Ardmore's wagon went on its way, Spencer did not miss the man, the ivory-handled revolver, or the gestures of goodwill. The A-J crew moved onward, joined with a couple of other outfits, each in turn, and continued the daily business of gathering, holding, branding, and tallying. After a few days going north, the crew headed west and crossed the country north of town. At the westernmost point it paused an extra day on a section of land belonging to Jerome, and then it made a gradual swing to the south. Town was almost due east, and Wingate's quarter section lay to the south. The roundup crew would pass on the western edge of that property.

Eva Wingate's rep presented himself at the wagon and traveled with it for four days. He was a quiet man of forty or so, below medium height, with dark circles beneath his eyes. His name was Orton, and he said very little about himself or the person who hired him. Though he paid attention and kept his tally, he did not assert himself. As a rep he did not have to stand night guard, so each evening he rolled out his bed not long after supper. Jerome treated him with the deference he allowed to all reps, but the two had only brief and functional conversations. After Orton left with his bed horse and the other three in his string, no one mentioned him or the last name of the woman he worked for.

During that part of the sweep, Spencer noticed that Jerome sent him and Trask out to the west each day to ride their parts in the circle. Other riders went closer to the Wingate homestead. One of them might have seen the remains of the brown horse, and one of them might have pushed cattle out of the grassy swale where Collins Wingate had died with a bullet in his back. No comments about any of that came to the wagon, though, and the crew made its final swing to the south and west.

Spencer leaned back against the slope of the tub, soaking in the warmth of the water. After six weeks of campfire smoke, burned hair, dust, and particles of dead vegetation, all carried on the wind and rubbed into his hair and clothes, one bath at the bunkhouse had not done the whole job. Now in the side room of the barbershop, with plenty of hot water and not just a couple of inches of lukewarm, he was feeling restored. Long days of work had left him strong and tanned, as if he had taken in the energy of the sun. Now he could relax, for a while at least, and enjoy the privileges he paid for.

After a final dunk, he raised himself from the tub and dried off his upper body. Then he stepped out and finished drying himself. He shook out his clothes and put them on. Though they had been clean when he left the ranch, they had picked up a bit of dust on the way in, and he wanted to preserve the clean feeling for a while longer.

Perkins and Trask were sitting in the main part of the barbershop when he stepped in and closed the door behind him. Perkins had just gotten his hair cut, and Trask had had a shave. As they stood up, Spencer caught a whiff of barber's tonic and bay rum.

"You boys smell like you're ready to go," he said.

Perkins waved his large-brimmed hat at waist level. "Let's git," he said.

Trask set down the newspaper he had just finished folding. "No one has to wait on him."

When they stepped out onto the sidewalk, the sunset was lighting the sky in the west. A horse and rider turned into the main street and came their way. Spencer recognized the shape of the man, then his separate details—the tall, dark hat with four dents and a peak in the crown, the reddish brown hair, the pointy upturned nose, and the dark brown clothing. He raised a gloved hand to his hired men and rode past.

Spencer and his two pals crossed the street. Just before they turned left to head for the Rawhide Saloon, Spencer saw Jerome turn in to the Paragon Hotel and tie his horse next to the palomino that Ardmore favored. It seemed normal enough. The two of them would probably take a small nook in the dining area, where they could drink a bottle of wine, eat a thick steak, and talk over the results of the roundup. Maybe neither of them would mention Farrow or Wingate, at least by name.

The interior of the Rawhide Saloon looked the same as it did the last time Spencer had seen it, six weeks earlier, though it had few patrons at the moment. Rex of the disappearing chin waited with his hands on the bar until the new customers spoke their request.

Trask looked over his shoulder. "I still don't like standin' with my back to the door," he said. "Let's go to the far end of the bar."

The other two agreed, and the group walked in that direction. Rex followed them with his eyes as he got their glasses and bottle ready.

"This is better," said Trask when the three had settled into place. "You can see both doors."

"Fine with me." Spencer laid a silver dollar on the bar top. "First round is mine."

Rex poured the drinks, and the three punchers lifted their drinks in salute.

"Here's to it, and them that can do it," said Perkins.

The other two nodded with "Yep" and "Here's to it."

"Well, here we are," said Spencer as the three of them set their glasses on the bar. "What shall we do?"

Trask tipped his head up. "We could take bets on who'll be the first to come through the side door."

A man who had been leaning on the bar turned and took in the group of three. It was Orton, the man with the dark circles under his eyes. "Hello, boys," he said. "All done for the time bein'?"

"That's right," said Spencer. "And yourself?"

"I finished my work. I'll be leavin' tomorrow or the next day. Got a job up in Montana."

"Well, I hope it works out well for you."

"So do I." Orton glanced around and said, "It's not always easy."

"That's for sure. But we try."

"Well, all the best to you boys." Orton turned and went back to his drink.

"Yup," said Perk. His dark brown eyes were wide open as he smiled and broke into a short verse:

I don't know, but I've been told,
The girls up there are awful cold—

Time flowed and the crowd gathered. Night had fallen, for no light came in from the open side door, nor from the front door when anyone entered there. A haze of tobacco smoke hovered. No one of notice had come in through the side door until Spencer and his pals were in their third round of drinks, when two women in feathered hats and flouncy dresses came in.

They paused at the far end of the bar, turned toward each other and exchanged a couple of words, and then separated. The one in dark hair stopped to chat with the first man she came to, while the other, a blonde woman with a powdered face, came toward the end where Spencer and the two others stood. She smiled and waved to men as she swung along, but it was evident that she was going to start at the far end and work back.

Trask spoke in a low voice. "Here she comes, Perk. If you want to go to the room with her, now's the time, before any of these mule skinners or ditch graders get their hands on her."

Perk's eyes were wider than before, and his mouth hung open. "How do I go about it?" he asked.

"You mean talkin' to her? Why, just like any other business, like buyin' a harmonica or a coin purse." Trask set his drink on the bar. "Here she is."

The blonde woman placed herself between Trask and Perkins, but even Spencer could see the exposed top of her bosom.

"Well, good evenin', boys," she said in a cordial tone.

"Evenin' to you," Trask answered.

"Which of you is the greatest gentleman?"

"Oh, that would be Spencer." Trask pointed with his thumb.

The woman leaned forward to get a clear view. "Are you Spencer?"

"I sure am."

"Your friends say you're a gentleman."

"That's because they're my friends."

She showed the tip of her tongue on her lower lip and then retracted it. "And you'd say the same of them?"

"I'd have to."

"Oh, then you're all full of sport."

"Don't leave out that young broncobuster there."

She turned to Perkins. "Are you a sport, too?"

"More a sport than a gentleman," he said with a blush.

"You might be both." She took his right hand. "What's your name?"

"Perk," he said, "as in Perkins. What's yours?"

"Belinda."

"I thought it was Ophelia," Trask put in.

She waved at him. "Oh, are you a naughty one?"

"Just sometimes."

She moved her left hand up Perk's arm, above his elbow. "And how about you, Perk? What are you like?"

"I'm a good boy."

"I knew it. I could tell right away. Not like these naughty ones. Are you a naughty boy, too, Spencer?"

"Nobody has ever told me I was."

She put her other hand on Perk's arm, between his elbow and wrist. "So, you like girls, Perk?"

"Oh, you bet."

"I wouldn't have let you tell me otherwise. You could never hide it." She touched the brim of his hat. "You've got a big hat. Do you wear it when you're bustin' broncos?"

"Most of the time."

"You ought to let me wear it." She laid her hand on his arm again. "But not in front of everyone else. Don't you think?"

She moved her shoulders, and Spencer was afraid Perk was going to fall headfirst into her bosom. By now she had shifted with her head turned away from the other two, so Spencer waited until Perk raised his eyes. Then he mouthed the words "How much?"

Perk frowned.

Spencer mouthed the words again.

Belinda turned and gave him a quizzical look, then directed her attention at Perk again. "What do you say, pretty boy?"

"About my hat?"

"Sure."

"I could let you wear it. Do you have a place?"

"Of course, sugar."

"How much?"

"Three dollars, Perk."

"That's a lot. I could buy three harmonicas with that."

"I don't know why you'd want to. You don't need but one, if that many."

"Okeh. Then I can give you the other two. Will you do it for two dollars?"

"Just for you, not anyone else." With her back turned to the other two, she took Perk's hand and gave him a little pull.

He held on to his hat with his other hand and let her lead him away from the bar. "Wait here for me, boys," he said.

"Don't worry," said Spencer. "Just hang on tight."

When the young cowpuncher and the saloon girl had gone out the side door, Trask tipped back his hat and said, "I hope that does him some good. Both the pleasure and the lesson."

"The lesson?"

"He'll find out how short it lasts. Damn near two days' wages, gone in fifteen minutes."

"Not a bad way to learn it, though."

"Oh, no. Some things are better to learn first-hand."

The two men lapsed into silence for a few minutes until the front door opened and Waltman came in. Two steps behind, Kern and Galloway followed and bunched up behind him as he stood surveying the crowd.

"There's High Hat," said Trask. "Him and his two foot soldiers."

Waltman's gaze came around to Trask and Spencer. The big man gave a toss of the head in recognition, then turned around and walked out with the other two following.

Trask shrugged. "I thought we might have the pleasure of his company."

"You get enough of him on the job, I take it."

"I'm sure I'm not the only one." Trask's tone of voice was dry.

"I wouldn't think so."

Trask raised his brows and peered at his drink without saying anything further.

Spencer took the lead in the conversation. "I notice he's been cool with you, doesn't have a lot

to say. He was that way with me for a few days
after I delivered that letter, but then he fell back
into his usual manner."

"I'd say you're right," said Trask, "as far as the
way he acts with me is concerned. He's had very
little to say, one way or the other, since the day I
told him he wasn't the foreman."

"He didn't enjoy that."

"No, and I think he's had it in for me ever
since."

"Had it in for you—in what way?"

Trask swirled his drink. "I think he'd like to get
me fired. Then he could feel that things were in
their right place."

"Has he done anything?"

"Oh, little things, all through roundup. Someone
leaves a rope on the ground, like from the horse corral, and he says, 'Oh, I think Trask was supposed
to pick that up.' Or someone misplaces a brandin'
iron, and he says, "I thought Trask had it last.' And
you know me. I don't drop things at my ass."

"I know. And it's just like him to say things
like that. With me, he likes to distort what I
say." Spencer lowered his voice and picked his
words, to avoid mentioning names. "Like he did
a couple of days after we found the body. That
whole incident left me soured on this place. The
boss acts as if nothing happened, the sheriff never
comes around to talk to us that found him, and
the man's wife is left to fend for herself." Spencer
glanced at Orton, who had his back turned and
was leaning into a conversation of his own. "So
after two or three days, I made a comment that
it wasn't a great joy to work in a place like this—

meanin' this area, not just the A-J. But right away he makes it into something different, like I was a turncoat. He said I'd be a fool to go off and throw in with the little ranchers, which I had no intention of doin' anyway. I told him so. I told him I wasn't a quitter and I'd stick it out through the season. I also made clear that it wasn't the A-J in itself, but this place in general, where dirty things happened and everyone looked the other way."

"What did he say to that?"

"Pretty much what you'd expect. He said you've got to take the good with the bad wherever you go."

Trask waved his hand. "Oh, well, to hell with him. I do my job and try to keep to myself. The less I have to do with him, the better."

"I agree with you there. As for keepin' to yourself, I think you've got that down better than the rest of us. Even when I try, it seems that things come to me. Take the last time we were in here. That fellow Anderson, he comes and chums up, and then later, a certain party wants to ride alongside us on the way home. Now, I didn't mind it, especially the second party, who was a friend of mine, and I think I've got the right to associate with whoever I please."

"I hope so."

"All the same, things like that get noticed. And they probably get reported more often than I'm aware."

"You shouldn't have to worry about that."

"I know," said Spencer, "but it makes you wonder what's in store for you when you've got friends who aren't in high favor."

Trask laughed.

"I meant those others, you know."

"Oh, I know. I was laughin' at myself—partly for not bein' in high favor, and partly for not havin' many friends. That's the secret to keepin' to yourself. But it doesn't prevent you from rubbin' someone the wrong way, especially when they try to high-hat you."

"That's the truth."

Trask paused and then tossed out a question. "So is that how long you're good for?"

"What's that?"

"The season."

"Oh, that part. Yeah, I'll work through the season, assuming that nothing interferes in the meanwhile, and then I can decide what to do next. How about you?"

"About the same. Like you say, if nothin' interferes."

Spencer realized their voices must have gone up a ways, as the man Orton turned and spoke to them.

"I'll tell you, boys, if you're ever lookin' for work, come on up to the Big Hole country, southwest of Bozeman there. I could help either of you get on."

"Oh, we're just talkin'," said Spencer. "We're all right."

"Maybe so, but the way things are here—now, at least—this wouldn't be a bad place to get out of."

"We get along," said Trask.

"Oh, I'm sure. But remember what I said. The Big Hole country. It's west of Bozeman and a ways south." Orton went back to his conversation.

A couple of minutes later, Perk came in through the side door.

"Well," Trask observed, "he didn't lose his hat."

Perkins walked the length of the bar and took his place with his two pals.

Spencer gave him a wry look. "Everything all right?"

"You bet," said Perkins, with a broad smile.

"What kind of harmonica do you expect to buy for a dollar? Silver and gold?"

"Oh, that was just the first thing that came to mind." Perk craned his neck. "I didn't notice the other girl when I came back in."

"Ready to go again?"

"No, just curious."

"She went off with another fella a few minutes ago," said Trask.

Spencer took a quick glance. "I didn't see that. Of course, I wasn't lookin' out for her."

"Neither was I. Just happened to notice." Trask paused in reflection. "I wonder if that was what Dick was bird-doggin'."

"Might be," said Spencer. "I assumed he was lookin' for the boss, but he may have just stopped for a peek in here on the way to the Horseshoe. I imagine those girls'll show up down there in a little while."

Movement at the side door caught his eye. Warren Robinson, the lawyer, walked in without pausing and took his place at the bar not far from the deer antlers. Rex pulled out the green bottle and poured him a drink in a wide glass. In his relaxed, unhurried way, the lawyer sniffed the surface of the liquor and then took a sip. Spencer recalled Wingate's word as he had waved to the lawyer on that earlier occasion. *Friend.*

Trask's voice brought him back. "We minded your drink for you."

"Thanks," said Perkins. "I didn't think about it much."

Movement at the side door caught Spencer's attention again. This time it was Wolf Carlton, whose dark gray hat, coat, and vest made a contrast with Robinson's lighter gray attire as Carlton passed within a couple of feet in back of the lawyer and took his place an arm's length away at the bar. Robinson took no notice of the other man, and Carlton showed no interest in the lawyer. Rather, the stock detective gave him the shoulder, standing straight up and turning away from the bar at a slight angle.

Carlton put his right hand on the bar, shifted as if he had put his foot on the rail, and called for a drink. Rex served him in short order. Carlton stood for a moment with a detached air, taking in the saloon. His round eyes, prominent cheekbones, and yellowish brown mustache gave him an impassive appearance. After his survey he looked at the drink in front of him, which he held between his thumb and first two fingers. He raised it, drank it down, and set the glass on the bar. Then he gave the rest of his back to Robinson and walked out of the saloon as he had done before, pausing just before he headed to the front door. No one said hello to him, and his eyes did not rest on anyone long enough even to tip a nod in greeting. All the same, Spencer was sure the man had a complete inventory of everyone in the Rawhide Saloon.

As Spencer watched the lean figure walk out the door, he said to himself, *Not a friend*.

Chapter Seven

The buckskin moved out of the ranch yard at a fast walk. Spencer reached forward and patted the animal's neck, then settled back and enjoyed the warmth of the morning sun. He had the feeling of freedom that came from a day off, and his attitude was improved with the knowledge that Waltman, his two foot soldiers, and Jerome had all stayed in town. At breakfast, Spencer had said nothing more than the minimum to Trask and Perkins—that he was going out on a ride—and they asked no questions. Mac had been in the kitchen, paying no more attention than necessary and perhaps sweetening his disposition for what he considered better company when the others came back from town.

Spencer rode north for a ways and turned off the main trail. He doubted that the others would be coming back this soon, but he preferred not to have to make any account at present; and besides, the distance would be a little shorter if he cut across on an angle to the northwest.

For as much as the plains country gave an illusion of sameness, it had quite a bit of variety for anyone who ventured into it. In addition to the usual rolling topography, the land had gashes and upthrusts that would be obscured half a mile off by a gentle hill. Spencer did not recall having traveled across this particular stretch of ground, and he observed it with the habitual attention of a range rider. At one place he came to a draw that narrowed into a tiny canyon. A green carpet at the far end, darker than the prairie grass, showed where a seep of water flowed.

Curious, and in no hurry, he rode toward the spot. When he was still a hundred yards off, he saw a dusky shape in the shadow of the canyon wall. He stopped. Letting his eyes rove on and around the object, he identified the dark forehead and chest of a deer. He made a small ticking noise with his tongue, and the animal tensed its ears. From the position of the mulelike ears, he could tell the deer did not have antlers, not even low-lying ones. A doe—maybe she had a fawn behind her. Spencer decided not to disturb things any more than he had already, so he reined the buckskin to the right and trotted up out of the draw.

The sun's rays were beginning to warm the air and glance back up from the ground by the time he reached the last small rise. He gave the horse a breather and took a minute to observe the house and stable. A couple of horses stood in the corral, but no smoke rose from the stovepipe. Spencer nudged the buckskin and rode down into the yard.

As he came to a stop, the corral gate opened and a woman led out a small bay horse and turned it around as she closed the gate. Spencer appreciated the features of the horse—compact, round-hipped, with a black mane and tail, a shiny reddish coat, and four white socks.

"Hallo," he called out.

Eva Wingate turned from sliding the latch. "Oh, hello," she answered. "I'll be right there." She made sure of the gate and led the horse forward.

Spencer dismounted and stood holding the reins. "Didn't mean to interrupt anything. Are you on your way somewhere?" Given her dress he didn't think so, but he didn't want to make assumptions.

"No. I was just going to brush him, but that can wait." She moved to the hitching rail, doubled the lead rope, and drew a loop to tie the horse.

Spencer noticed that she was wearing a full-length, dark blue dress with a low collar and plain sleeves, which showed her shape to advantage. Her dark hair was let down and tied together in back. When she turned to face him, he said, "I had a little time to spare, so I thought I'd drop in to see how you're getting along."

"That's thoughtful of you," she said. "I'm doing well enough, I suppose. Considering." She frowned, then raised her hand to shade her eyes.

He moved a quarter turn, and the horse shifted around behind him. He tipped his hat so the brim blocked out the glare.

She moved accordingly, lowered her hand, and spoke again. "I didn't know if I'd see you again."

"Oh, really?"

"Most everyone has seen fit to stay clear." Her blue eyes steadied on him. "And besides, I thought you might have considered me a bit un-appreciative the last time we spoke."

"Not at all. I just imagined you saw me as not doing much, and I could see a reason for it."

"Well, be all that as it may, I appreciate your stopping by." She gave him a pleasant smile.

Not sure of what to say next, he began with "I met the man you hired, Mr. Orton."

"I thought you would. His report was not so detailed as to include the names of everyone he met, though." She smiled again, and her demeanor was relaxed.

"Of course. But did he do all right for you?"

"I suppose so, but it's hard for me to judge. He seemed reliable, but I don't know how much he exerted himself."

"He wasn't very pushy, from what I saw."

She gave him a reserved look as if he had made a small joke. "At any rate, on the basis of the report he gave me, it seems as if we've lost cattle. I'm not sure what to make of it."

Spencer wondered about her use of "we," but he brushed past it. "Cattle—would that be cows, calves, steers? If you ended up with quite a few cows without calves, it could be that someone got to the calves ahead of time. If you lost cows, then maybe someone did away with them and kept the calves."

"Mercy. How do they do that?"

"Variety of ways. One is to kill the cows for beef, and another is to leave 'em go to waste. If they do it that way, takin' the cow and calf together, they usually pick on pairs where the calf hasn't been branded yet. They sacrifice the cow for the sake of gettin' the calf. Of course, they can change brands, too, but however they do it, they're not likely to put their brand on a calf and then let it go back to its mother with her original brand. Wherever you seem to be down in the count, that might tell you something about where your losses came from, or how they came about."

"But it won't get me the cattle back."

"Probably not." Then he amended by saying, "Actually, not at all, if they've done away with some and branded the others."

She gazed off in the distance, then came back. "My impression is that I've lost mother cows, which would mean, most likely, cows and calves. Orton said he didn't see a great many cows without calves."

"That matches with what I saw, and he would have no reason to give you incorrect information on that."

"Would he on something else?"

"Oh, I think he'd have to be deeper into it to be covering up for someone else. Did he speculate on what might have caused any losses?"

"Perhaps to himself, but he just gave me the figures and left it to me. I didn't tell him ahead of time how many I was expecting, but I did tell him afterwards that I had thought it would have been more. He didn't have much comment. He said that was the count and he thought it was pretty close."

"It probably was." Spencer met her eyes for a few seconds. "I don't suppose you've gotten an idea from any of the other small operators as to how they've done."

"They've kept to themselves. As I told you that day in town, I believe, Collins tried to convince them to stick together, but they chose not to. And I'm sure they've been busy with their own interests." She glanced away, knitted her brows, and said, "Actually, one of them came by, but it was not to offer help or to talk about the state of affairs."

"Oh?"

"A man named Bates. Perhaps you know him."

"Only at a distance. He has a place northwest of town."

"Had."

Spencer frowned, then relaxed his expression to let her continue.

"As soon as he got his stock gathered, he sold out everything—horses, cattle, and homestead."

"Really? He's done that in the last three weeks, then."

"That's right. He didn't care to say who bought his holdings, and I don't believe he would have taken the trouble to call, except that he wanted to sell me some chickens. He said they were good laying hens, and his wife had done well with them. I believe he thought he was being gener-ous and helping me out."

"His notion. So he's gone, then?"

"Pulled out, to use his expression. I can't say I admire him for coming around with that sort of gesture of friendship after turning his back on my husband, but I don't blame him for wanting to save his own neck."

Spencer smiled at her not mincing her words, but rather than add to it he said, "We helped him make some of his gather, and he didn't seem threatened at the time. Maybe he was playing it close to the chest. Or better yet, playing it safe."

"That seems like it."

"By the way, I understood that this lawyer fellow, name of Robinson, was handling George Farrow's estate, settling his affairs. I wonder if you might get some support from him."

She arched her eyebrows in an expression of skepticism. "One finds out who one's friends are," she said. "Collins thought he could count Mr. Robinson among his friends, but I've gone to see him, and he's been very noncommittal."

"I'm surprised. I thought that in taking on Farrow's business he was showing a little—"

"Courage? Maybe so. But he's done it in full view of everyone, with the backing of the law, and when the place is sold—that is, the property and the livestock and all—he'll collect his fee. With all respects to Mr. Robinson, I think he is honest or mostly so, but he looks out for himself."

Spencer reflected for a moment. "Well, at least someone is paying for these places, not just moving in and taking over outright—though I imagine they would if they could. Next best, I imagine, would be to push someone out and buy him cheap. I'd guess that's what Al Jerome has done with Bates. Jerome has got a section of land next to Bates up there, so I'd bet he's the one who has bought it. He can use Bates's well and buildings to control that part of the range a little easier." Spencer studied Eva's face, as she seemed to follow him with interest. "Who do you think is in line to buy Farrow's place, then?" he asked. "Ardmore?"

"I wouldn't be surprised. He seems to have acquisitive as well as inquisitive tendencies."

Spencer laughed. "You seem to have gotten a glimpse of his character."

She gave a wry smile. "He's been so good as to come by."

"I didn't mean to—"

"Not at all. Please don't feel there's anything discreet—not on my part, at least. He drops by once in a while, under the guise of helping me out, but he has his innuendoes about the lonely widow, and so on. He's a great friend of Mr. Jerome, isn't he?"

Spencer reflected and then said, "By all appearances. Why would you wonder?"

"Oh, I'm not sure. But it seems as if one doesn't always know which side he's on. He has the markings, as you say here, of a landgrabber, and yet he makes comments hinting that I should beware of Al Jerome wanting to buy me out."

"Sounds as if he wants it for himself."

"It could well be, with a little sweet-talking just for fun. But I wonder about his sympathies. Collins was sure that he and Jerome were thick as thieves. In cahoots, he called it."

"I don't doubt it, but that wouldn't keep Ardmore from trying to do the best he can for himself." Spencer paused for a second and added, "You say he's inquisitive."

"That he is. And more about financial matters than anything else—though he makes sure I understand he's looking out for the poor helpless widow."

Spencer twisted his mouth and then spoke. "I can't say it surprises me much, except, as you say, his passing unfavorable remarks about his—"

"Confederate. There, you didn't put yourself in a position."

"I hardly think you'd quote me."

She laughed. "No, you're right about that." Her eyes settled on him. "But tell me what you know. I've been doing all the talking, it seems."

"I don't know a great deal. They don't say much around me. But my impression is that these confederates, as you call them, wanted to make a move and expand their holdings. They've weakened a couple of places, to put it mildly, and they've put the fear into a few other small-timers, to make the acquisition easier. I realize I'm not telling you anything that you haven't already told me. Furthermore, it's hard to prove any of this." He paused, received a nod from her, and went on. "As for what comes next, it's hard to guess. If it turns out that each of these two fellas acquires new property, then we can expect something more to happen. Maybe they'll compete for this place, or maybe the friendly one is just trying to soften you up, and they're still in cahoots to work together on it."

"Well, that's interesting."

Spencer did not have anything definite to add, but he thought she did, so he waited for her to say more.

"Is there anything you've got in mind to do? You gave me the impression before that you might find a way to, well, do something."

He gave a light shrug. "As I said then, I'm going to keep my eyes and ears open." Even as he spoke, he knew his comment was inadequate, and he could see impatience in her face.

With a sharper tone than before, she said, "I would wonder to what purpose. You've already said you haven't learned much that way."

He met her eyes and did not find much help there. "I'd like to get the goods on these fellas, just like you would," he said. "But if we can't do that, maybe we can keep them from doing any more."

"How? No one stopped them from getting Collins. But of course, you're not obliged to do anything."

This last comment set him back even more than the previous two. "I don't know," he admitted. "But I think Ardmore is the one to watch."

"What about the other one?"

"Jerome?"

"No. The one Collins mentioned. The one he called Wolf."

"Well, um, my idea is that you don't go looking for him. Maybe someone can trace something back to him, but as for someone doing something that—"

She frowned. "I'm sorry, but this sounds rather vague. Do you really hope to achieve something, or is it just goodwill?" Then she added, "Not that there's anything wrong with that."

His spirits fell. "To tell you the truth, it is pretty vague. I want to help you, but I don't have much more than that in mind."

"Help me do what?" Her tone was serious, not criticizing.

"Well, for one thing, I want to help you not lose your place. I don't think anyone's going to do any physical harm to you. That's already been done, though not to you, of course. I think they'll try to push you out, and we need to thwart them."

"How?"

"I don't know. Be ready for them, I guess."

Her face softened, and her blue eyes now seemed to hold sympathy for him. "This is kind of you, Mr. Prescott," she began.

"Please call me Spencer."

"Very well. Spencer. As I was saying, this is very kind of you. Considerate, thoughtful. And I appreciate it. Your friendship." She took a deliberate breath and went on. "For what it's worth, I believe you're one person I can trust. I thank you for that, and I thank you for stopping by. Please feel free to do so again."

She gave him what he could only think of as her best smile, which supported the sympathetic expression in her eyes. He understood that she did not believe he could do anything.

"Thank you," he said, touching his hat. "I expect to." He led the buckskin a few yards away and mounted up. When he turned to look at her, she had begun to untie the bay at the hitching rail. He waved at her, and she waved back. He admired her posture as she looked over her shoulder that way, and he understood well enough why Ardmore might be attracted.

Spencer gave the cinch one more pull, buckled it, and let the stirrup down from where he had flopped it onto the seat of the saddle. He walked the dun out a few steps, checked the cinch for tightness, got the reins in place, and climbed on. With a touch of the spur, the dun left the ranch yard at a trot.

The noonday sun had Spencer riding on his own shadow. In the week since he had seen Eva Wingate, this would be the third time he went on the lookout, and he hoped the afternoon proved better than the morning. He hadn't thought to ask her whether Ardmore came on some particular day of the week or at some usual time of day. On his first two attempts, both at midmorning, Spencer had kept watch from behind a row of bluffs about fifty yards long and the height of a boxcar. The ground sloped up on the backside where he hid, so he picketed his horse down behind him and lay on the springy grass, peering over the crust of tan clay with a pair of field glasses.

He didn't like spying, and he didn't like the feeling of dishonesty that came with shaving his schedule in order to sneak off for a while. But he believed what he said to Eva Wingate, that Ardmore was the one to watch. He couldn't have told her why, except that the smiling man seemed to get around more than Jerome and seemed to be playing both sides of the game. Spencer's notion was that if Ardmore came again to visit Mrs. Wingate, something might happen not long after that. For all Spencer knew, Ardmore had already made a call when Spencer was not at the lookout. There were many hours in the day, especially now in summer. Nevertheless, Spencer followed his hunch. At the same time, he decided that if he didn't see Ardmore today, he would drop in on Eva Wingate as soon as he could, to find out if anything had happened.

When he reached the low bluff that he used as his observation point, he noted that the sun was up at his right shoulder. That much agreed with him, as he would have less glare as he looked through the binoculars. On the other hand, he was in for a near smothering, as the air on a hot day was much heavier close to the ground than it was when a fellow sat up on horseback.

He settled into place and waited. As before, he convinced himself that this was the best spot. Less than a mile from the Wingate homestead and about a mile from the main trail, it over-looked the route that anyone would take from town, Ardmore's, or the A-J. So even if Ardmore came the long way around, dropping in for col-laboration with Jerome, he would most likely come by here.

Time crawled. Each time Spencer looked up, the sun appeared to be in the same place. Mean-while, the heat was sinking in. His face was sweating, and his shirt was sticking to his back. The ground felt warm to the touch, and the buffa-lo grass, never lush, itched as it was beginning to wither and curl in the heat of summer. Bits of dry grass clung to the sweaty backs of his hands.

He felt restless and pinned down. He had to get up and move around, for no matter how short a time. After taking a long look at the rangeland below, he was sure no one could pass through his field of vision in less than three, four min-utes. He pushed himself backward and rose to a crouch, then moved downhill and let the rim of the bluff close off his view. Standing up, he took off his hat and fanned himself with it as he walked the rest of the way down the slope.

He patted the warm neck of the dun horse, felt the heat on the shiny saddle leather. In the presence of the horse, he felt a twinge of conscience. Here he was, in the middle of a vast landscape, watching out for a man who might not pass by, while others might well be watching him. He shook off the feeling. He had come here for a purpose, and he was going to stick with it for a while.

After fanning himself one last time, he set his hat on his head and moved uphill, crouching as his eye came even with the rim. Down on all fours, then on his elbows, he stretched into position and took the field glasses from where he had left them.

Sweat came to his face again. He flicked a small black ant from the back of his left hand. A snuffle came from the dun horse. He turned and scanned the area downslope and saw nothing out of order. On his stomach again, he took up the glasses and searched the grassland.

A dark spot appeared in the east, dark and light together, moving against the pale green background. Focusing on it, Spencer determined it was a man on a light-colored horse. He lowered the glasses, then raised them and peered again. It looked like Ardmore on his white horse, the one that he favored along with his palomino for traveling back and forth between roundup camp and home. Ardmore of the dark suit, coming along at no great hurry under the wide sky.

Spencer put down the glasses and waited. No need straining his eyes for something he should see well enough in a few minutes.

Horse and rider came closer. Ardmore sat relaxed in the saddle, his hat tipped forward and his rein hand swaying loose above the saddle horn. The white horse was moving at a fast walk, faster than it had seemed at first. Spencer did not move as the pair approached. Small puffs of dust rose from the horse's hooves, the hem of the rider's coat waved, the hat bobbed. Spencer held his breath as dark and light passed in front of him, less than four hundred yards away. Ardmore raised his arm, wiped his brow, and settled his hat in place. The white horse switched its tail, and then Spencer saw the bottoms of its shod hooves as the animal moved off to the right.

Spencer let out a long breath and lowered his chin to rest on his hand. He turned onto his side and looked downhill, where the dun stood dozing with his head forward. The countryside all around was as empty as before. Spencer reached for the glasses and pulled them to him, and with a sense of relief as if he had just crawled out of a hole, he went down the hillside in springing steps. He tucked the field glasses into the near side of the saddlebags and the picket pin into the other, and after leading the dun about fifty yards, he checked his cinch and mounted up.

Breathing free, he set out north in the direction he had been heading to begin with. He had had a little delay, but he was back in his routine and not up to anything that would attract attention.

He tipped his hat on one side for ventilation and drew his sleeve across his brow. The dun picked up its feet and bounced along. The sunlight came down at his left, but it felt comfortable, not stifling as before.

He rode on. Ardmore would have arrived at the Wingate place by now, would be smiling and congenial, maybe brushing his coattail aside to show his ivory handle.

That was enough to think about there. Spencer turned his thoughts to the country ahead, the route he was to take and the brands he was to look out for. Thinking back, he realized he hadn't seen any cattle since before he took up his observation point. He ought to come across some pretty soon.

The trail ahead curved to the left to go around a bluff like the one he had used for his lookout, except that this one was not much longer than a single boxcar. He followed the trail, glancing at the clay rubble at the foot of the bluff and wondering if there were any snakes there.

As he turned his eyes to the trail in front of him, he felt a jolt in his stomach. Sitting on a dark horse and blocking the trail at the edge of the bluff was Wolf Carlton.

Spencer rode forward, edged off to the right side, and stopped when the horses' heads were a couple of yards apart.

"Afternoon," came the man's somber voice.

"Same to you." Spencer's throat was dry, but he thought the words came out all right. He put his left hand on the saddle horn to steady it, and he kept his right in plain view, resting on his thigh. As he waited for Carlton to speak again, he took in the man and his horse at a glance.

Carlton was dressed as on the previous two occasions Spencer had seen him. Topped with a dark gray hat that had a single crease running lengthwise, the man wore a jacket, vest, and pants of a similar color. The hat sat firmly on his round cranium, and in the shade of the brim his round eyes and solid cheekbones gave way to a narrowing of the face with the yellowish mustache prominent. The mouth moved.

"Travelin'?"

"Ridin'. Out on my day's work."

Carlton gave him a thorough looking-over and asked, "Do I know you?"

Spencer was sure the man did, but he answered straight, "My name's Spencer Prescott. I ride for Al Jerome, of the A-J."

"I see."

Wondering what more the detective wanted, Spencer added, "I'm out checkin' the range, seein' how the cattle have drifted since roundup."

"Nothin' wrong with that. Have you seen much?"

"Actually, I haven't, not for the last little while. But that's the way they are."

Carlton gave a thin smile and spoke in a dead, level tone. "Sure."

"Anything else?"

"I don't think so. I assume you're going a ways north, then coming back around to the home ranch?"

"That's right. Just as I was told. I hope there's nothing wrong." Spencer let his eyes drift for a

second, and he noted that in spite of wearing a
jacket, Carlton did not seem to have sweated at
all. Maybe the man had been waiting in a cool,
shady place.

"Oh, no," said the detective, his tone easier
now. "I don't mean to seem too curious, but it's
my business to know who comes and goes on
certain men's properties."

"I understand."

"Nothin' to it."

Spencer wondered if Carlton meant there was
nothing to understanding or nothing to the simple work of knowing who came and went. Meeting the man's eyes, he said, "I suppose I can be
on my way, then."

"Of course." Carlton gave a small nod and
moved his horse forward and off to the side.

As he did, Spencer got a better view of the
man's horse and outfit. Carlton rode a dark
horse with no white markings, and he used a
lightweight, single-rigged saddle with a low
horn and cantle and hardly any skirts. Beneath
the man's knee rode a smooth leather scabbard
with a rifle stock showing.

Spencer touched his hat brim and rode by, letting the dun pick up its feet and move out in a
trot. He did not look back at the stock detective,
but he had plenty to wonder about. This was a
big country, and Wolf Carlton might have several things to keep an eye on. For some little while
at least he had been watching Spencer. The man
had not taken on a threatening air, but it gave
Spencer a chill to think that Carlton might have
lurked behind him as he kept an eye out for Ard-

more. On the other hand, Carlton might have seen him for the first time just a few minutes earlier. In any case, Spencer might be on the man's list of people to observe out here—along with Eva Wingate, perhaps, or even Ardmore.

Spencer rode on in the warm sunlight, but the chill stayed at his back for quite a while.

Chapter Eight

The smell of fried bacon hung in the air as Spencer took his seat at the breakfast table. Waltman had gotten there a little earlier and now sat in his usual place, smoking one of his thick, uneven cigarettes. He had his right elbow resting in his left palm, and his right hand held the quirly in the pose that some men would hold a cigar or cigarillo. Waltman seemed absorbed in thought, as he squinted in the tobacco smoke and gazed across the table toward the wall. His rough complexion, thick features, and short, coarse hair gave him the appearance of a tomcat as much as ever, and his pensive aspect made it seem as if he was contemplating the apparition of a large field mouse from the world of dreams.

Perkins took his seat at Waltman's left and across from Spencer. "Smells like lard," he said.

"It's bacon." Waltman's voice sounded a bit hoarse.

Galloway sat down across from Jerome's empty seat and began handing out cups. Mac showed up with the coffeepot, set it down in front of Galloway, and went back to the kitchen.

The door opened, and Jerome came in. He hung his hat on the peg and sat in his usual place. The coffeepot came to Waltman, who poured a cup for himself and one for the boss. Kern took a seat, then came Trask, and the table was complete.

Mac appeared with a platter of fried potatoes. Jerome dragged some off for himself and handed the dish to Waltman.

"Everyone can go out as they've been doin'," said Jerome.

Waltman raised his head and passed the plate to Perkins.

The boss spoke again. "Except you, Spencer. I've got a separate little job for you."

Mac appeared with a plate of fried bacon, which he held as Jerome served himself. Then the plate went down the other side of the table, beginning with Galloway. Waltman paid no attention to the food but turned to listen to the boss.

Jerome continued with what he was saying. "You remember the Bates place, up north?"

"Sure." Spencer took the plate of bacon from Kern.

"Well, it's part of the A-J now. He was supposed to have vacated, and I need someone to take a look and see what condition he left the place in. I want to use it for a line camp, so I need to know if he left bunks, a table, and a stove like he said he would. Also, see if the corrals and barn need any work."

"Did he have a barn?"

"He called it that. It's more of a shed, but I still need to know if it's in order."

"All right."

"Take two horses—one to ride on the way up, and the other for the ride back. Put your bed on the second one, and get a bait of grub from Mac. Stay the one night, and be back by dark tomorrow."

It sounded like a full schedule, but nothing troublesome. "I'll do that," said Spencer.

Waltman, who had been fixing a vacant stare on the table in front of him, said, "Then you don't want me to go on that trip."

"That's what I thought yesterday," the boss answered. "But I decided it would be a good job for Spencer. You can ride with me down to Alderman's. I want to see how he cuts hay." Then with his voice a notch higher he said, "Can you think of anything you need, Spencer?"

"Not at the moment. Sounds pretty uncomplicated."

"It ought to be."

Spencer picked out the dark horse for the first day's ride. No amount of riding seemed to be too much for the horse, as it was always ready to run out from under Spencer. After getting the first horse saddled and ready, Spencer brought out a husky sorrel that matched the other one for size and that in Spencer's estimation shouldn't give any trouble leading or packing. He decided that for as little as he was taking along, a regular riding saddle would be easier than a packsaddle and britching, so he brought out a well-worn company saddle that no one used and put it on the sorrel. A short while later, with help from Trask, he had his pack tied on and was ready to go.

Trask stood by after helping him with the lashes. The quiet puncher looked over the second horse and nodded.

"Thanks for the hand," said Spencer. "See you tomorrow."

"Don't mention it. Have a good trip."

The dark horse, which did not act up when there were other horses around, settled into a plucky walk. The sorrel fell in beside and half a length back. The day had a good start to it, as the sun had been up for an hour and a faint breeze blew out of the west. Spencer relaxed in the saddle and went with the rhythm of the horse's movement.

Thinking about the road ahead did not take long, and when he had it mapped out, he took to thinking about the task itself. He wondered why the boss had changed his mind from sending Waltman, and he thought it might be Jerome's way of pulling Spencer out of his usual pattern and keeping him from loitering in the vicinity of the Wingate place. The boss might also have someone on the lookout today, as he would have Spencer's departure timed. Well, that was easy enough to deal with. Spencer decided he would ride straight through today, as he was supposed to do, and then if he got a good early start on the way back he could take a cut-across route and see if Eva Wingate had anything new to mention. If Jerome had someone on the watch tomorrow, Spencer might ride around him and come into the A-J ahead of him. That could be amusing in itself, though Spencer would probably not know the results unless someone came trailing in late or out of humor.

For the time being, however, he did not see any complications. He followed the trail north, passed up the turnoff that led west into the Wingate place, and kept north until the trail was about to curve to the right to follow the gap through the buttes. Out on the other side, the trail would turn north again to

go into town, or a rider could take the turnoff east
to go toward Farrow and Ardmore. Even though
Spencer was not going that way today, he pictured
it in his mind as a way of placing himself. Then he
took a trail that led off to the left, angling northwest. This trail, as he recalled, would go around the
buttes on the west side, straighten out to go north,
and cross the main road west of town. From there
it would continue north and take him to the Bates
place and the adjacent section of Al Jerome's.

Riding into the yard of the homestead, Spencer could
see that the place was abandoned. At his right the
little house stood alone, with no children or dogs or
cats, not even a rag hung out to dry. The windows,
what few there were, had a gloomy and gaunt cast
to them. A few white chicken feathers fluttered
where they were caught in the weeds, and behind
the house a low heap of white-and-dark manure
showed where the chicken coop had stood. Across
the yard to the left, a larger heap of sun-bleached
brown manure reminded Spencer that Bates had
kept a few head of cattle and a couple of horses
close in. Spencer recalled seeing the Bates kid during roundup—a skinny kid in nester clothes, riding
a swayback roan with no saddle as he herded in a
milk cow, a yearling heifer, and a bull calf.

Straight ahead, past the house and the two manure heaps, sat the shed and lean-to that had been
referred to as a barn. The lean-to ran the length
of the front side of the shed, and the area beneath
consisted of hard-packed earth with a few chicken
feathers caught in rough spots. Within the roofed
area, a set of coyote ears had been nailed above the

doorway to the shed itself. The door was closed, but it hung so crooked that Spencer assumed it had spent much of its existence hanging open on its leather hinges. Before he dismounted, he rode to the end of the shed and gave the corrals a looking-over. The rails were holding up though they were a motley collection of planks, poles, and in some places branches. Some pieces were nailed, while others were tied with rawhide or lengths of discolored rope with broken ends.

Spencer turned the horses around, brought them to the hitching rail in front of the shed, and dismounted. After tying the horses, he went into the shed. It was a dark place that smelled of axle grease and dust, and he could see that the open doorway provided the only source of light. As his eyes adjusted, he made out a couple of rough-hewn saddle racks and a grease-stained workbench.

As Spencer went back out into the daylight, he reflected that Bates had taken every scrap of wire, rope, chain, lumber, and iron. At least he hadn't used the saddle racks or workbench for firewood before he left. Some men would have, along with wood from the corrals.

Spencer unsaddled the dark horse, then unloaded and unsaddled the sorrel. There was not a wisp of hay around, so after brushing the horses he picketed them out on the grassland. He thought about taking his bedroll into the house, but he didn't know if any lice or bedbugs had stayed behind to meet new company. He had brought the canvas ground sheet he used for roundup and any other time he slept out, so he decided he would roll out his bed under the lean-to later on.

Still casting around to gather impressions, he walked to the house and opened the door. The interior did not smell musty yet, just stuffy from being closed up in hot weather. It did not take him long to explore the house. The front door, which looked west out onto the yard, led into a front room with a kitchen on the left side and a sitting area on the right. A sheet-iron stove squatted against the wall on the north end, an unpainted table and two spindly chairs sat in the middle of the room, and two wooden bunks not much more elegant than the workbench occupied the two corners at the south end. Beyond the front room, the back area was divided into two bedrooms, both empty.

In the front room once again, he sat on each of the wooden bunks to test them for stability. He did the same with the two chairs, and he rested his elbows on the table. After that he checked the sheet-iron stove. It looked like the type a man could put his foot through after a few years of use, but the sides as well as the stovepipe felt solid. The firebox was half-full of ashes, and a six of clubs lay on the wooden floor beneath the center of the stove, but other than that, Bates and his family had left the place picked pretty clean.

It gave Spencer something of an empty feeling to be looking over this place where people had lived and longed, worked and hoped. A faint spirit lingered. It would vanish, he imagined, when range riders made this into a line camp—when spurs would scratch the floorboards, nails would be driven into the walls for hanging chaps, bacon grease would spatter on the stovepipe, and tobacco smoke would blend with the smell of leather and grease and melted candles. For the moment, though, he caught a sense of the people who had left this place behind.

Although that sense haunted him in a small way, he realized he would much rather be here than in George Farrow's house, where the late tenant did not have a chance to clear his things out. Spencer imagined one of Ardmore's men, maybe the one whose name was Crow, walking around inside that house and noting how it could be put to use.

Spencer went to the lean-to, where he unpacked his bundle. He didn't want to roll out his bed yet; not only did he wish to avoid inviting a snake to get in ahead of him, but he also wanted to use the bedroll as a seat. Keeping it rolled up, he set his war bag on the ground in front of him and took out the cold biscuits and beef he had packed along. The sun was slipping in the west, and the air was still. Not a sound came from the ranch yard, nor from the rangeland around him. A few flies showed up when he took out the food, but he brushed them away and did not waste time with his grub.

When he was finished eating, he walked out and moved the horses, even though the grass had been grazed close everywhere near the homestead. He returned to the lean-to and rolled out his bed as the last rays of sunlight faded. As he pulled off his boots he thought he would try to get an early start on the next day, but that was tomorrow. For right now, things were uncomplicated as he had hoped.

In the gray light before sunrise, Spencer gathered the horses and brought them to the corral, where he pumped fresh water into the wooden trough and let them drink. Two cold biscuits and a slug of water made his own breakfast. He had brought along a can of peaches, which he could have eaten the night before and used the can to boil coffee this morning, but without a scrap of firewood he wasn't going to make even a little squaw fire in the yard. The can of peaches would stand him in good stead at noontime.

He saddled the two horses, loaded the pack onto the dark horse, and tied off the load. The sun had cleared the hills in the east when he rode out of the yard of the Bates homestead, now the A-J line camp. A mile out, he heard a meadowlark, which together with the clip-clop of horse hooves made the music of a new morning.

Al Jerome had told him to be back by dark, but with the assumption that the return trip should take about the same amount of time as the trip north, Spencer figured he could ride into the A-J at least two or three hours before that. For travel time, Jerome might have been thinking in terms of going through town, as he himself might do. A man could figure three hours from the A-J into town, and five hours from town to the line camp, but in a direct route he could cover the distance in an hour less.

Spencer gave it another moment's thought. Maybe Jerome assumed a rider would go through town because that was the way Waltman had said he would go. On the other hand, maybe Jerome was giving Spencer enough time to go out of the way and be seen doing it, as Spencer had imagined the day before. Now, with a closer idea of the actual travel time, he still wondered about the boss's motives. Whatever they were, Spencer knew one thing: Jerome was no fool.

Spencer crossed the main road leading west from town and continued south. At noon he stopped and ate the can of peaches while the horses took a breather. An hour later, when the trail started to veer to the southeast, he kept going south by southwest, which he figured would bring him in due north of the Wingate place. Allowing for a short conversation there, he didn't think he would add any more than an hour to his total riding time for the day. Everything should be all right.

Eva Wingate was sorting through a bundle of burlap sacks when Spencer rode into the ranch yard. She was wearing a pair of trousers and a loose shirt, which did not detract from her appearance as she stood up and brushed stray hair away from her cheek. Her blue eyes sparkled as she looked at her visitor.

"I wish you'd been here fifteen minutes ago," she said.

He swung down from the sorrel. "Really? Did something happen?"

"Not much. I had quite a time of it getting these sacks down by myself. Collins had them hanging from a rafter inside the stable there."

"Oh. Do you think you'll need some help getting them back up?"

She smiled as she brushed at her hair again. "One benefit I got out of doing it myself was that it gave me something to think about. And my conclusion is that if I hang them in a place where I don't have to risk my neck just to put them up, I won't have such a hard time getting them down by myself the next time."

"Good thinkin'." He nodded in reflection. "Then you're not packin' up to leave."

She flicked a glance at the dark horse. "No, but it looks as if you might be."

He gave a light laugh. "Oh, no. I was just off on an errand where I had to camp out for the night. The boss sent me up to the Bates place to look things over. Seems he bought it, which is no surprise. Anyway, I saw where Bates had moved out and taken every last straw with him."

"That's all right for him," she said. "But I'm not ready to go yet."

The shine of her eyes and the spunky tone of her voice brought a smile to his face. "That's good to hear," he said. "Have you got any news from your far-flung neighbors?"

She gave a wry expression that he was becoming used to, and she said, "The ardent Mr. Ardmore has been back, but he hasn't made any more advanced offers or declarations. Just questions and hints and innuendoes, very much like before."

"I see. Well, I wouldn't want to fall into the same category, but I must confess I just dropped by to see how you were doing and to ask if you need any help. I don't have anything new to report—nothing I've heard or seen, nothing I've done."

Her eyes took on a soft shine, which he was also becoming familiar with. "Don't feel that you have to apologize," she said. "I realize I may have made you feel you should be doing something. But as I said before, you're not obliged to. And I do appreciate your stopping by. It's thoughtful and considerate."

From her tone of voice he did not feel he was being dismissed. He glanced toward the burlap sacks, which she had been separating into piles. "Is there anything I can help you with, then?"

She laughed. "I'm going through these bags because I have a little time on my hands, and I thought I would sew up any that have holes in them. I doubt that it's your kind of work."

He smiled in return. "You'd be surprised what some punchers can do with needle and thread. I've patched a few things."

A smile played on her face. "I'm sure you have. But I assume you've got better things to do now than to go through a stack of burlap."

"As far as that goes, you're right. I should be getting back to the ranch. I detoured this way to see how you're doing, and if I don't delay too much, it would be just as well."

"Don't be in too much of a hurry," she said. "At least water your horses."

"I can do that."

She walked along as he led the horses to the water trough. There he loosened the front cinch on each saddle and let the horses drink. Neither he nor the woman spoke, and the only sounds were of the animals taking in water and then of the drops falling from their muzzles.

When he thought the horses had drunk enough, Spencer moved them back from the trough and tightened the cinches.

"I guess I'll be goin'," he said, moving the horses out of the way and then pausing to meet her eyes.

"Like I said, feel free to drop by when you want." With a smile she added, "If you have more time at the next visit, I can get you a needle and thread."

"I'll look forward to it." With a touch of the hat brim he turned and led the horses out. After setting his reins and making sure the lead rope was clear, he swung aboard and got the horses going together in the right direction. As he turned to see how the pack was riding, he lifted his eyes and saw Eva Wingate standing in the middle of the ranch yard. He waved, and she waved back.

Spencer rode into the A-J well before sundown. He left his bed and war bag in the bunkhouse, and as he unsaddled and put away the two horses, Jerome and Waltman came riding in from the south. Spencer gave the boss a report on how things looked at the Bates place, and Jerome seemed satisfied.

"You made good time," he said.

"Oh, I did all right."

Kern and Galloway came riding in on a slow walk. Before dismounting, Galloway spoke to Waltman. "Say, Dick, did you sleep in a feather bed?"

Waltman raised his head. "We slept in Alderman's bunkhouse. They loaned us some blankets."

"Well, things were pretty quiet around here," said Galloway as he swung down. Turning to Jerome, he said, "I guess that's just as well, isn't it, Al?"

"That's right, Scot." Jerome gave his hired man a smile of approval.

Even with a full table once again, supper was not a very boisterous affair. Mac had cooked a pot of beans with bacon, along with four tin plates of biscuits. The men spoke little as they clacked their spoons on the crockery dishes and ate their grub.

After the meal, Galloway and Waltman each pushed away from the table to roll a cigarette. Al

Jerome did not leave as he often did at this time but rather sat in his chair and said nothing. Kern took out a plug of tobacco and performed his dexterous feat of cutting off a chew without trimming off the tip of his nose. Jerome watched with an expression somewhere between impatience and dislike. Perkins and Trask went to their bunks, but Spencer kept his seat, as he thought the boss might have a few more questions about his trip.

None came, however, and Spencer was about to get up and go to his bunk when the front door opened.

Jerome sat straight up and said, "Come in."

A bulky figure stepped inside and came forward. As the man moved into the lamplight and took off his hat, Spencer recognized the features of Sheriff Ross. He was a stout man, dressed in clothes the color of charcoal—a gray shirt beneath a spreading wool vest of darker gray, almost dull black, which in turn was covered by a full-cut wool jacket. He had graying hair, a full mustache not yet gone to gray, and a puffy face. As he scanned the table and then settled on Jerome, his pale blue eyes had a prying, searching quality.

"Care for supper?" asked Waltman, lowering his cigarette.

"Not quite yet, thanks." The sheriff redirected his gaze straight at Jerome and said, "I'm here on bad news, Al."

Jerome frowned. "What kind?"

"Cliff Ardmore has been killed."

"What?" Jerome's voice rang out, and then his fist banged on the table. "I say, there's been enough of all of this!"

The sheriff blinked. "I'd say so, too."

Jerome heaved out a breath as if he was trying to get control of himself. "Well, when did it happen?"

The sheriff pushed out his mustache, brought it back, and said, "I put it around four o'clock this afternoon. That's after talkin' to his men—and his wife, of course."

Jerome nodded. "I see. And where did it happen?"

The sheriff cleared his throat. "About half a mile east of the gap, on the trail that goes from his ranch to the place where this other trail comes out of the buttes."

Jerome shook his head. "You don't know if he was coming or going?"

"No, I don't. He was seen at about two o'clock in town, and he didn't go back home, so he must have gone south of town. He could have been looking around out there, or he could have gone through the gap and come back."

"How do you fix the time at about four, then?"

The sheriff wheezed a breath through his nostrils. "One of his men found him at about half past four, and he hadn't been dead all that long."

"I don't like this at all," said Jerome.

"Neither do I." The sheriff's pale blue eyes traveled around the table.

Now Waltman spoke. "Do you think someone was layin' in wait for him in the gap there?"

"It's hard to tell, but it looks as if he was shot from up close, out in the open, so it was likely someone he knew. That's just a first impression, though."

"Huh," said Jerome. "Around four o'clock. Dick and I would have been coming back from

Alderman's then. We went down there yesterday and spent the night." He seemed to give it more thought. "Spencer, though, might have been coming through there at about that time." He turned his head. "What about that, Spence? Did you come through town, or did you come down around the other side of the buttes?"

"I stayed west of town goin' both ways."

The sheriff turned where he stood to let his pale eyes bear down on Spencer. "Where were you?"

"I went to the Bates place, which is now part of the A-J. I went up there yesterday, spent the night, and came back today."

"Is that right?" said the sheriff. "Chances are, you could have seen or heard something. At about what time did you come down the west side of those buttes?"

Spencer hesitated. "Well, as a point of fact, I didn't stay right on that trail, so I would have been a ways west of there, and at least an hour earlier in the day."

Jerome gave him a sharp look. "What way did you come, then? You got in just a little ahead of us."

Spencer moistened his lips. "I veered west where the trail angles southeast. I came by way of Wingate's. I stopped in to water the horses and see how the lady was getting along."

Jerome's eyes were cold as he said, "That was considerate of you."

Spencer did not answer.

The sheriff's eyes bored in on him again. "You're Prescott, aren't you?"

"Yes, I am."

"You're the one that brought in Wingate's body."

"That's right. Dick Waltman here was with me, he and another man, when we found Wingate dead."

"And you're the one that paid a visit to Cliff Ardmore's wife a while back."

Spencer's pulse jumped. "I was carrying a message from Al Jerome to Cliff Ardmore, and the lady invited me in. I wasn't there but a few minutes. It was a mistake. I've already been called on it, and I was on speaking terms with Cliff Ardmore after that."

The pale blue eyes put him under scrutiny again. "I don't think I'm spillin' any secrets," said the sheriff, "but Cliff Ardmore thought someone might have been seeing his wife. For all I know, that's what he was checking on when he was shot."

"I'll say this," said Jerome. "Cliff didn't make enemies. He was friends with everyone."

The sheriff breathed with his mouth open as he turned to the owner of the A-J. "That's what everyone says. Now I've got it boiled down to two motives. One, someone thought Ardmore had a hand in the deaths of a couple of other men, and this someone was trying to get even. Two, it was something more personal, such as an interest in the man's wife."

"Well," said Jerome, "Spencer has been friends with some of these little ranchers and their men, but I don't think he would take it that far." He tossed a glance at Spencer and then returned to the sheriff. "As for his whereabouts this afternoon, from what he says, they vary a little from what I would have assumed."

Spencer felt all eyes on him as he answered. "I'll make it clear," he said. "I had nothing against

Cliff Ardmore, and I was miles away from those buttes at four o'clock this afternoon. You can ask Mrs. Wingate. She can tell you herself that she was sorting out a bundle of grain sacks when I came by. We exchanged a few words out in the yard, I watered the horses, and I went on my way. Figure the time from there to here, and I think you have my whereabouts pretty well accounted for."

The sheriff bunched his mouth and then said, "You seem to make ready friends with the wives of other men who turn up dead."

Spencer could feel his blood coming up. "You've got a way of putting things together," he said, "but if I was trying to get somewhere with one woman, I wouldn't be off waylaying the husband of another."

"Unless you didn't like him seeing Mrs. Wingate."

Spencer felt a jolt. "What does that mean?"

The sheriff shrugged. "Oh, just that it was known that he had gone to see her a couple of times."

"You must know more about it than I do, then, but in any case, I think you can peg down where I was. Not only that, but I had a packhorse taggin' along, even if I had tried to be in two places at the same time. I'll show you the two horses, and you can tell me if you see their tracks there, or through the gap, or anywhere other than where I've said I've been."

The sheriff's eyes narrowed in his puffy face. "Don't get too wound up," he said. "I came out here to do two things—deliver some unwelcome news, and find out if anyone knows anything. I don't jump to conclusions. Now, if you don't mind, I'll ask each of these other fellas if they saw anything when they were out and about."

Spencer went to his bunk and stared at the ceiling as the sheriff questioned Kern, Galloway, Perkins, and Trask. Spencer could hear voices, but he did not pick up specific questions and answers. When Perkins and Trask had both come back to their bunks, Spencer asked if anyone had anything new.

"No one saw anything," said Perkins. "But the sheriff did say one thing that was interesting."

"What was that?"

"Cliff Ardmore's ivory-handled pistol wasn't on him when they found his body."

"Well, I sure as hell don't have it," Spencer said. "They can search me."

"No one wants to," said Trask. "They know they wouldn't find it."

As he tried to go to sleep that night, Spencer had plenty to wonder about. If he had to pick a suspect for Cliff Ardmore's death, he would select Wolf Carlton. After all, there was no league of smaller ranchers, and no one was going to take it upon himself. But Carlton could well have done it. He got out and around, and even if he wasn't seen in public with Ardmore, he was rumored to be working for the bigger cattlemen and probably knew him well enough to ride up close. As far as that went, Carlton could get close to anyone he wanted, even if he preferred to use a rifle from a distance. Like the sheriff, though, Spencer didn't want to jump to conclusions. He speculated on the possibility that Carlton might have had an interest in Mrs. Ardmore, but the idea of Carlton being a womanizer didn't fit.

Spencer was stuck for a motive. If Carlton had done it, what would have been his reason? Why would he, to use Waltman's phrase, bite the hand that fed him? Maybe it was nothing personal. A man like Carlton didn't need a motive. He did his work for pay and probably for the satisfaction of having done it. That was the simplest and most logical explanation, but it still left the question of who would have a reason to hire such a job to be done.

Chapter Nine

Perkins brought in an armload of firewood and set it by the cast-iron stove. With the weather getting cooler now, the men had a fire for a while each evening. After supper, those who didn't go to their bunks would pull their chairs over to sit by the stove, which took up a space against the north wall between the sleeping area and the eating area. This evening, all the men but Perkins had drawn up a chair, though Spencer didn't expect Trask to stay very long. He never did.

"Gaw look out fer spahders," said Kern, who sat by the door of the stove. From time to time he opened the door and spit in, to save himself the trouble of going to the front or back door of the bunkhouse.

"What's that?" said Perkins as he stood up.

"Spahders. Good way to pick one up."

"Oh, spiders. You bet I'm careful." Perk walked out the back door to fetch more wood.

"I had a brother," said Galloway, "got bit on the end of his peter by a spider. He was about a year old, I guess. I wasn't old enough to remember it, but they say it swelled up like a balloon."

"That'll do it," said Waltman, as if his confirmation made the story legitimate.

Kern spit into the fire. "You say you *had* a brother. Did somethin' happen to him?"

"Oh, no. He's still alive. Last I heard anyway."

Spencer caught a glance of Trask, who sat at the edge nearest the bunks. The dark eyes moved to each man who spoke, but Trask showed no reaction.

Waltman spoke again. "Some spiders can kill a man."

"Black widdas," said Kern. "And they hang out in farwood."

"Then you don't want to go danglin' your peter there," said Waltman. "What's wrong with you, Trask?"

"Nothin'. Why?"

"You looked as if you didn't like what I just said."

"Didn't notice. Must have been the thought of spiders."

"They say you kill a spider, it's goin' to rain," said Galloway. "Isn't that it?"

"They say a lot of things," said Waltman. "If I see one I mash 'im, or burn 'im with the coal of my cigarette. Same with snakes, I tell you. I kill every one I can."

Galloway spoke again. "Al said you killed a hell of a big one the other day, out by the buttes."

"Oh, yeah. Comin' back from town. Big around as your arm."

Galloway had rolled up his shirtsleeves before supper and had not rolled them down yet. His wrist and forearm were spindly, half as big around as Waltman's. "How long?" he asked.

"Maybe five feet. Al said I should take it home and skin it, but I didn't want to haul that ugly-smelling thing all the way back here."

"How'd ya kill it?" asked Kern.

Waltman seemed to swell a little with pride. "Pistol shot, right through the head."

Galloway rolled down his right sleeve. "What did Al say?"

"He was glad I killed it."

Trask got up and went to his bunk. Spencer would have gone, too, but he took some interest in the telling of the story. Ever since Ardmore had been killed, Al Jerome did not go anywhere alone. Sometimes he had Galloway ride along, but most of the time Waltman sided him, and Galloway seemed to envy the status.

Perkins came in with another armload of wood. He set it on the stack and pulled a chair to the spot Trask had left open. "Still talkin' about spiders?" he asked.

"No," said Galloway. "Snakes."

"Oh. That's a lot better." Perkins smiled and sat down.

Waltman took out his tobacco and papers and began to build a cigarette. No one spoke for a minute, and then he said, "I guess a couple of you boys'll be goin' up to Bates."

"To Bates?" Perk asked.

"The line camp."

"What's there to do up there?" asked Galloway.

Waltman had his brows raised and his lids half lowered as he looked down his nose at his work. "I think Al wants the crew to lay over there for a night or two during fall roundup, and he wants it to be ready." Waltman grabbed the tag with his teeth and pulled the string. "You went up there, didn't you, Spence?"

"Of course I did."

Waltman leaned back and slipped the bag of tobacco into his vest pocket. "What do you think needs done?"

"I don't know. Maybe lay in some firewood."

"In that country?" said Galloway. "I don't know where you're goin' to find it. By the way, Dick, who's he gonna send?"

Waltman did not answer until he finished rolling the cigarette and licked it. "I couldn't say. But it'll be sometime in the next few days, and he'll tell us then."

Al Jerome did not hold his men in suspense for very long. The next morning at breakfast, as he poured molasses on his hotcakes, he said, "I need two men to go up to the Bates place to get it ready. Come fall roundup, I want to use it a couple of days, and after that we use it as a line camp." He looked down the table. "Spence, you've been up there once and know the layout. Perkins can go with you."

Spencer nodded in agreement. He was surprised Jerome didn't send Trask with him, as that was how the boss often did it when he sent men out in pairs. He would have Kern and Galloway work together, unless he took Galloway with him, in which case he might pair Kern and Waltman. He sometimes had Waltman work with Perkins, or even with Spencer, which would leave Perkins and Trask together. Through these various combinations, he just about never had Waltman and Trask together, and yet that would be a logical pairing if Perkins went with Spencer. Maybe Jerome planned to go on another short journey with Waltman, leaving Trask as an odd man out. That would work, as Trask was something of a loner anyway and never seemed to mind being sent off on a job by himself.

Jerome continued. "Take four horses—the two you ride, and two more. Pack your beds, some grub, and something to cook with. Figure on stayin' three nights. That'll give you two full days of work while you're up there. First off, fix anything that needs it on the house, the shed, or the corrals. Take along a hammer, some nails, and a saw. You finish around the place, then you lay in some firewood. Or you'll probably need some firewood first."

"That'll take a little doin'," said Spencer. "Nearest wood is on Clay Creek, about two, almost three miles away."

"Here's the way you can do it, I think," said Jerome. "You pack a load of cut-up wood on each of the two spare horses, and you drag something more with your saddle horse. You get back to the place, you chop up what you drag, and you stack it all inside out of the weather. If that stove is good enough to cook on, the firewood'll go a lot further there than in a campfire. But we'll still need a pretty good stack if we cook for a whole crew for a couple of days."

"All right," said Spencer. "We'll get in as much as we can."

"Sure. Take an ax for each of you. I know it's not the easiest way to bring in firewood, but it would be way too slow to send a wagon all the way up there and back." The boss smiled. "But I'll tell you this. We'll appreciate it when we get to that point in the roundup."

"That's a bet," said Waltman in his deep voice. "There's times your bed gets damp and don't dry out for a couple of weeks, especially in the fall. That place could be just the ticket."

Jerome spoke again. "That should do it, then. You shouldn't have any trouble. By the way, pack about twenty pounds of grain for the horses. You say the grass isn't very good right there." After a pause he asked, "Have you got any questions?"

"I don't think so," Spence answered. "How about you, Perk?"

"Sounds fine."

"That's good," said Jerome. "You can get a start right after breakfast."

Spencer and Perkins made good time and crossed the main road west of town in the early afternoon. The sky was overcast, and the weather was cool with a breeze blowing out of the west. At the crossing, Spencer dismounted and unwrapped his coat where he had it rolled up in his slicker behind the saddle. The coat was of tan canvas with a wool blanket lining, and he appreciated the warmth right away when he put it on. Then he rolled up the slicker again and tied it in place with the saddle strings.

Perk did not have a slicker, so he had less work getting out his jacket, which was blue denim and also had a blanket lining. He smiled as he put it on and shrugged into it. It made him look more filled out, and his brown hat with the tall dented crown and large brim did not look proportionally so large.

"I'm just thinkin'," he said, as his broad upper lip twisted into a smile. "It's not too late in the day, and we're not very far from that road ranch I've heard tell of, are we?"

"It's about halfway between here and town," said Spencer. "Less than three miles, I'd say."

Perk raised his eyebrows in a question. "What do you think? We could drop by there and still make it to camp by nightfall, couldn't we?"

"I think so, if we don't get stuck there for a long time."

Perk opened his eyes in a wide, good-humored expression. "How long does it take?"

"Depends on who you're with. I've been with fellas that once they get in a happy mood, they don't want to leave. 'Just one more,' they say."

"Oh, I don't care about the drink. Maybe have one. But you know the rest. When you're done, you're done."

"Sure. I've got no objection. A little detour, a little time there—maybe add an hour and a half to our trip. We can go from there up to Bates, not have to come back this way."

"Well, let's go, then," said Perk. "Not waste time. Those girls'll be there this time of day, won't they?"

"At the road ranch? Oh, yeah. They live there."

With the wind at their backs, they made it to the Blue Horse Road Ranch in less than an hour. It was a long, low, wooden building with a hitching rail long enough for a dozen horses. Not a single animal was standing there at the moment, though, so Spencer and Perkins did not have to crowd their four horses as they tied them.

Inside the Blue Horse, Spencer let his eyes adjust to the dim interior. It had been a while since he had visited the place, and the previous time had been at night after a dozen drinks, so the dull daytime atmosphere made the establishment seem different from the joint he had known before. Spencer was not surprised to find the bar along the left wall, though he had not had that detailed a picture in his mind before he and Perkins walked in. Against the back wall sat two divans, both of them dull and frayed. Along the right wall stood an upright piano with a circular stool in front of it. The center of the room was unoccupied, and Spencer had a dim memory of men and women dancing there. Right now, however, no one else was present in the room.

Movement at the back corner beyond the bar caught his eye. A drab curtain hanging in a doorway parted in the middle, and a short, round-bellied man came through and took his place behind the bar.

"Afternoon, gents," he said in a subdued voice. "What can I favor you with?"

As Spencer and Perkins stepped to the bar, the curtain moved again, and a heavy redheaded woman with a scarcely contained white bosom came out. Spencer noted her and turned to the barkeep, who could have passed for the woman's brother, as he was also red-haired, at least around the fringe, and pale.

"We'll have a glass of whiskey," said Spencer.

The roly-poly man bobbed his shiny head and came up with a bottle and two glasses. "Here you go," he said. "Just what you need on a day like this."

Spencer laid a silver dollar on the bar. He assumed the man would say the same thing in any season, and from the looks of him, he might not get out to check the weather very often. The man had bulging eyes and faint eyebrows, with a splotchy complexion that ran up and over the curve of his dome. In addition, he had a protruding mouth with thin lips, and Spencer would not have been surprised if the man had snapped at a fly and caught it.

Now the woman spoke, her voice as silky as that of a woman fifteen years younger. "Hello, boys. What are you up to?"

Perk gave her an indifferent look and said nothing, so Spencer answered. "I came here to prop up my pal in case he goes weak in the knees."

She looked Perkins up and down. "Why would he do that?"

"He's like the tigers in the story. Turns to butter."

"I don't remember that story very well," said the red-haired woman. "What makes him do that?" She eyed Perk again.

"Girls," said Spencer. "Especially yella-haired ones."

"I should have known," said the woman. "Your good luck is, we've got a couple of girls, haven't been here long, that fit that description." She walked to the curtained doorway and called into the back region of the building. "Hey, you, Bertie and Imogene, come on out. There's a young fella here, hasn't been weaned long, and he looks like he's about to faint."

Two girls came into the saloon area, both of them with hair the color of wheat straw. That was their first and last point of resemblance, however. One was short and buxom, while the other was taller than average and shapely without spilling out of her dress. They walked past the two punchers, turned around, walked past the other way, and stopped.

The buxom one looked at Perkins as she spoke. "Which of you two is about to faint?"

"Neither of us," said Perk. "My pal just likes to exaggerate."

The round-featured girl moved toward Spencer while the more slender one approached Perkins. Spencer smiled, and although he didn't show interest, the chesty girl went on in her forward manner.

"You boys need someone to pull your boots off, don't you?"

Spencer motioned with his head toward Perkins, who was already speaking in a low tone to the other girl.

"What's your name?" he asked.

"Roberta," she answered. "What's yours?"

"Perk, as in Perkins."

The girl near Spencer called across, "Is it perkin', then?"

Perk looked at the girl next to him and said, "It might be."

She smiled and said, "You don't look like you're gonna faint at all."

"Don't feel like it, either."

"What do you feel like, then?" The girl had a soft glow in her brown eyes as she spoke.

Spencer thought that if the places were switched, he might not resist with that girl. But the one he had drawn had a coarser appeal, and he was able to stick with his plan of not going to the room with any girls today.

Perk answered, "I feel like I'm sittin' on a real twister, and they're about ready to take the blinds off."

The girl put the tip of her finger on the ridge of Perk's belt. "Do you want to go in back, then?"

"To the room?"

"Sure. To my room."

"How much?"

"For you, Perk, just two dollars. Or five dollars for all night."

"Oh, I can't stay that long," he said. "Let's do the short go."

"Whatever you like." She took his hand and led him away.

The girl by Spencer's side said, "There. You see? He's got the pants for it." She rolled her eyes across Spencer. "How about you, sugar? Don't you think you'd like to?"

Spencer shrugged. "Not much in the mood today."

Her tone relaxed from trying to be seductive. "Why don't you buy me a drink, then? Be a gentleman."

Spencer assumed the bartender would pour her a drink from a different bottle, but he thought he should be a good sport, so he said, "All right."

"Arly," the girl called out. "One for me."

Sure enough, the bartender pulled out another bottle and poured a watery brown liquid into a glass for the girl. He retrieved the change he had left earlier.

"Thanks," said the girl, raising her glass but not drinking from it. "What's your name, darlin'?"

"Spencer."

"That's a kind of gun, isn't it?"

"A rifle. What's your name?"

"Imogene."

"That's a nice name."

"Sometimes I think I'd like to change it. Too many humorists in the world. 'You're a what?' they say, or 'I thought you said you were a queen.' And others."

"I'm not that quick," said Spencer.

"Oh, I don't know," she replied. "I heard what you said to Madge before she called to us. But you're a good sort." She set her drink glass on the bar after barely touching it with her lips. "Well, I've got to go, Winchester. Maybe we'll see you again."

"Sure," he said. "Thanks for the company."

"Thanks to you. For the drink."

Spencer did not follow her with his eyes as she walked away and passed through the curtained doorway. Madge had disappeared, and Arly the bartender had sunk back on a stool. Spencer took a sip of his whiskey. This place was okay. With the exception of girls cadging the price of a drink, a fella paid for what he wanted, and he got what he paid for. Perk would be coming out in a little while.

The clouds had rolled in closer, bringing cold, damp air. About an hour after Spencer and Per-

kins left the Blue Horse Road Ranch, a drizzle
started to fall. After riding in the light rain for
a ways, Spencer stopped his horse and untied
his slicker.

"Wish you had one, too," he said to his pal.

Perkins wore a broad smile. "I'm fine."

"Stoked your fire pretty good, did you?"

"Oh, yeah."

They rode on through the wet afternoon. Mois-
ture collected on the front and hind quarters of
the horses as well as on the canvas-wrapped
packs. Spencer could see that Perk's denim jacket
was taking in the dampness.

"I say," he spoke out. "I think this canvas coat
of mine sheds the water better than that one of
yours does. How would you like to wear this
slicker for a while?"

"I'm fine," Perkins said, like before. "Once
you're wet, you're wet. No reason for both of us
to get that way. How much farther is it, do you
think?"

"Oh, a couple of hours, maybe."

"That's all right. Once we get there, we've got
a good dry place to hole up in."

"I don't know how much of a fire we'll have
tonight."

"No matter," said Perk. "We'll be fine."

"Your own fire still burnin' all right?"

Perk smiled. "You bet."

The late afternoon was darkening into evening
when the wet outfit pulled into the Bates place.
Spencer went into the house first, as Perk held
the horses, and he was glad to find the whole
place dry.

The men took the packhorses to the doorstep, one at a time, and unloaded everything into the front room. They put the packsaddles on the floor along the front wall, and the bedrolls went on the two wooden bunks. The smell of dust mingled with the smell of wet canvas and sweaty pads.

"Let's unsaddle the other two and put that stuff in here as well," said Spencer. "Then we'll put all four in the corral and give 'em some grain."

The corrals were divided into two sections. The men put the horses in the near one, where grain troughs were nailed onto the wall of the shed. Perkins spread out about five pounds of grain as Spencer went to look at the other section of the corral.

Coming back to where Perk stood by the horses, Spencer said, "I think we can borrow a few branches off that back corral, where they've got it patched up. When we drag in some more, we'll fix it like it was."

"How about this?" Perkins shifted the sack of grain that he held.

"There's a bench inside the shed where you can leave it."

The branches were wet and night was falling when the men got back into the house. Spencer lit two candles and looked around for the hatchet they had packed. He caught a glimpse of Perk, shivering.

"Why don't you get out of that wet coat?" he said. "Get into something dry, and I'll see if I can get a fire going."

By candlelight he broke off the narrow ends of the branches, which were mostly wet, and set the pieces on the floor to dry. Then he used the hatchet to split the thicker pieces. It was slippery, clumsy work, much better done on a chopping block outside if the weather were dry and if there were such a block. After a while he had a small heap of dry chips and splinters and chunks. He fetched a newspaper from the gear, and he laid a fire on top of the old ashes in the sheet-iron stove. He lit the paper and stayed crouched, waiting, as the fire took hold. The flames were pale and low, and they warmed as much with the appearance of a fire as with the heat itself.

Perk had changed into a dry shirt and was wearing his wool cap with the little bill. He set a chair with its back to the stove and hung the sodden coat on it. "For as much good as that'll do," he said.

Spencer used the back of his hand to fan air into the fire box, but he raised ashes more than he brightened the fire. "Pretty slow," he said.

For supper they ate cold meat and biscuits. Spencer continued to fuss with the fire, but he couldn't build it into a hearty blaze.

"It's not that cold in here," said Perk. "And the beds didn't get very wet at all. It'll be all right."

"Sure," said Spencer. "But a better fire would help." He glanced at the wet denim. "You probably want to get a slicker before fall roundup, don't you?"

"Oh, yeah. I had one before, and I don't know where it went. But I'll get another one."

"We'll see what it looks like when we get ready to leave. Maybe we can go through town on the way back." Spencer held his palm toward the fire and felt a bit of warmth. "Unless you feel compelled to drop in and see your girl again."

Perkins gave his broad smile. "Roberta? I'd hardly call her my girl. And, no, I don't have to get back right away. Plenty of time for that."

In the gray light of morning, Spencer had to build the fire all over again. He thought the ashes were too deep, but he didn't have a shovel and couldn't think of a handy way to clean them out, so he left that job for later and built the new fire on top.

As the first small flames began to rise, Perkins came to stand by the stove. "This thing's still pretty wet," he said, laying his hand on the denim coat. "I was thinkin' of goin' out to give the horses a little more to eat."

"Wouldn't be a bad idea," said Spencer. "When we get to where we're goin' we can stake 'em out. I hope the grass is better there than it is here." He blew on the fire. "I want to get this goin' well enough to boil some coffee, and if I do, it might dry out your coat a little."

"I'll go see to the horses, then."

Spencer looked up. "Take my coat. It'll be cold out there, damp as it is."

"Nah, I don't need it."

"Take it, so you don't come in with the shivers." Spencer got up and handed him the tan canvas coat.

"Oh, all right." Perk took it and put it on, fastened two buttons, and went out the front door.

Spencer crouched by the stove again and was laying a dry splinter on the low flames when the report of a gunshot sounded outside.

He rocked back on his heels in surprise, then caught his balance as he rose to his feet. He listened and heard nothing. Taking light steps, he went to the front door and cracked it open. As he looked out, he saw nothing but cold, damp morning. Then he made out the shed, the corner of the corral, and a horse coming to poke his nose over the top rail.

Spencer opened the door wider, and as he did so he heard hoofbeats dying away to the south. "Perk!" he called. "Perk! Are you all right?"

Then lowering his gaze, he saw that Perk was not all right. The young man lay on the ground in front of the door of the shed.

In a matter of seconds, Spencer pulled on his slicker and went out the door. Crossing the yard, he looked all around and saw nothing. Then he came to his young friend who lay sprawled facedown in the dirt.

A hole had appeared in the back of the canvas coat, and a red stain had spread a couple of inches across. Spencer knelt by the body and turned it over, limp and sagging, onto its back. A larger stain of red, as big around as a dinner plate, had already colored the front of the coat, and Perk's face had gone pale.

A dozen thoughts came to Spencer all at once. Someone had shot at the tan canvas coat, not at the young man wearing it. If Perk had been wearing his own coat, if it hadn't been raining, if he had had a slicker, if they hadn't detoured to the road ranch, if he had been wearing his large, dark hat, if he had come out wearing anything but Spencer's coat—a thousand ifs, and none of them doing a bit of good. Perkins had caught a bullet meant for Spencer, and his life had gone out.

Spencer raised his eyes and looked around. Nothing but this, the horses moving in the corral, the set of coyote ears nailed to the wall above the doorway of the shed.

Still kneeling, he put his left hand beneath the back of Perk's head and laid his right hand on the kid's still-warm cheek. "I'm sorry, Perk," he said, choking on his words. "I'm sorry. There's no way to make this right, but I will do something."

Chapter Ten

Sheriff Ross leaned forward in his seat and glanced across his desk at Spencer. The lawman seemed to be practicing his technique of boring into the person he was interrogating. His puffy face shifted in grimaces of agitation as he asked questions and listened to answers, but his pale blue eyes held steady.

"Your friends don't have very good luck," he said.

"It was Perk's bad luck to be wearing my coat," replied Spencer, "but the shooting itself was no accident. It was planned, same as it was with Collins Wingate."

The sheriff pushed out his lower lip. "You think the same man did both of 'em?"

"I don't know, but it's likely. Same style. Shoot 'em in the back."

"There's a couple of differences," said the sheriff.

"Bound to be some."

"For one thing," continued the sheriff, "you and two others found Wingate. But in this case, there was no one else around but you."

"There was the person who fired the shot."

"Well, all right, but my point is, I have to take your word for the whole thing."

Spencer could feel the anger coming up. "What do you think, that I had something to do with it? Perk was a friend of mine, a hell of a likeable kid. Furthermore, I had just lent him my coat."

"All the same, the cases are different. In one, a man gets killed out on the range, probably in the afternoon. In the other, it happens right outside the house, in the morning."

"Like George Farrow."

The sheriff's mustache bristled as his mouth shifted around. "A second difference is that Wingate, and you can put Farrow there as well, was part of one element. It's no secret that there was a feud brewin' between these little ranchers and a couple of others, who had 'em pegged for rustlers."

"I don't like the sound of that."

"I'm just summarizing what someone else has thought or said. Let me go on. By theory, at least, Wingate and Farrow were killed for being on one side of the feud. Cliff Ardmore was on the other. Now, your boss, Al Jerome, has told me several times that he thinks the other side got Ardmore out of spite, to get even, and he also told me he thought they'd try to make a move against him or one of his men. If you think there's anything to that idea, goin' tit for tat, then the Perkins kid is different from Wingate because they're on different sides."

"And where am I?"

The sheriff gave Spencer a few seconds of study. "To tell you the truth, I see you as bein' in the middle. Friends with Wingate, but workin' for Jerome."

"Well, that bullet was intended for me. I'm sure of it. And whoever lined up his sights on the back of my coat could easily be the same one who lined up on Collins Wingate. On top of that, I don't think the little ranchers ever came together on any kind of a plan, so I don't see this as two sides takin' it out on each other."

"Sounds like you've got an impartial killer in mind."

"Maybe he gets paid to be."

"You've got a lot of ideas, Prescott. To give you the benefit of the doubt, I'll just say they don't all coincide with mine. But I do believe you about the way this Perkins kid got it. Seemed a few minutes ago that you thought I didn't."

Spencer waved his hand. "It was the way you phrased it, but you were makin' a different point anyway."

"Just a matter of bein' skeptical. I have to be." The sheriff glanced at the window and came back with his pale blue eyes on Spencer. "Your boss isn't going to like this at all. I assume you're on your way there now."

"Pretty soon. I have to buy another coat, and then I'll go to the ranch."

The sky was clearing when Spencer stepped out of the mercantile wearing his new sheepskin coat. He would have preferred a coat like the one he had just lost, but the sheepskin was the only thing close to his size. Once outside, he was glad to have it. This cold, damp weather in the latter part of September was usually followed by a clearing out and then a frost. The way the air felt on his face, he thought a freeze was pretty likely.

He went to his horse and smoothed out the slicker where he had left it draped over the saddle. He set Perkins's dark hat and denim coat in the center and folded the slicker up and around to make a bundle, which he tied onto the back of his saddle. Then he untied both horses and mounted up. He gave a deliberate look at the barbershop, touched the brim of his hat in farewell to Perkins, and led the horse with the empty saddle as he rode out of town.

Al Jerome's face showed great surprise when he opened the door and saw who was standing there.

"Spence! What are you doing back here already? And where's Perk?" The boss looked past Spencer, craning his neck as he took in the two horses at a glance.

Spencer thought the boss might invite him in, but Jerome made no such move, so Spencer spoke from where he stood. "I've got bad news, sir. Someone shot Perkins in the back."

"The hell!" Jerome's face tightened as he focused on Spencer. "What for? Where were you? Was this some fight in a saloon or whorehouse?"

Spencer shook his head. "No, sir. It was right there in the yard of the Bates place. Perk went out to feed the horses while I stayed inside to try to get a fire going, and someone shot him square in the back."

"This is no good," said Jerome, still looking cross as he tightened his jaws. "What would anyone have against him? He was such a likeable kid."

"That's what I say. But I don't think anyone meant to kill him. You see, he was wearing my coat and that little wool cap of his."

Jerome frowned.

"His coat had gotten wet," Spencer continued. "I told him to wear mine. When he went out, it was still early, and cloudy as well, so there wasn't much daylight. I think someone took him for me."

Jerome's eyes went over Spencer. "I see. That's what's different. You've gotten a new coat, haven't you?"

"I had to. The other one was ruined. Bullet hole front and back, and terrible bloodstains. I don't think I could have worn it again anyway."

"I don't imagine." Jerome's eyes met Spencer's. "What did you do with Perk?"

"I took him to town. I told the sheriff what happened, and then after I bought this coat I came out here. I figured you should know as soon as possible."

"You were right about that."

"I left the rest of the gear there, plus two horses. I guessed you'd still want someone to do that work. Maybe Trask could go back with me."

"I might have to think about that. Nah, I'll tell you what. You can plan on goin' back up there yourself. Otherwise we'll be too short-handed around here." His gaze went vacant for a few seconds, and then he said, "This is just a lot to have to think about all of a sudden."

"Yes, it is."

Silence hung in the air for a couple of seconds until Jerome said, "Go ahead and put the horses away. This is a hell of a thing to happen to that poor kid."

"Yes, sir." Spencer heard the door close behind him as he walked away.

When he was finished with the horses, he went to the bunkhouse, where Kern, Galloway, and Waltman were sitting around the stove. From the way the place went silent when he opened the door, Spencer could tell that the other men had already heard the news and had been talking about it.

Waltman had a cloudy expression on his face as he turned toward Spencer. "Al said the kid got killed."

Spencer glanced at the three men, who seemed to resent his presence. "That's right," he said. "Early this morning."

Waltman gave him a hard stare. "Where were you?"

"I was inside, trying to get a fire going. He went out to take care of the horses."

"Al said he was wearing your coat."

"That's right. His was wet, so he wore mine. I don't think anyone meant to kill him."

"But they did all the same." Waltman's lip curled. "Trouble just seems to follow you around."

"Blame it on me if you want," said Spencer, "but I don't know how much of it was my fault if someone was lookin' to shoot me in the back but got someone else by mistake."

"You don't sound very sorry." Waltman raised his tomcat head and wagged it each way about an inch.

Spencer felt a jump in his blood. "There's no good way to talk about this, but I'll tell you, I was damn sorry, kneelin' next to him and knowin' he got shot instead of me. I liked that kid as much as anyone, and you know it." He flicked a glance at

Kern and Galloway, who were keeping quiet. "By the way," he said, "where's Trask?"

The room went silent until Waltman answered, "He's not here anymore."

Spencer frowned. "Not here? What does that mean?"

Waltman looked up from studying his finger-nails. "He got found with a runnin' iron under his saddle skirts. You know what that means."

It meant the same as saying a man was a rustler. Spencer had his doubts. "Who found it?" he asked.

"It doesn't matter," said Waltman. "He got found out, and Al won't stand for it. He told Trask to roll his blankets this morning."

Spencer was silent for a moment. Just the day before, he had counted on Perkins and Trask sticking up for him if need be, and now they were both gone. He was on his own.

Waltman had gone back to clicking his thumb-nail against the nail of his middle finger. Spencer would have bet a good sum that Waltman had found the running iron, and given the would-be foreman's animosity toward Trask, he might have been the one who put the iron there as well. Now it made sense that Trask hadn't been picked to go along with Spencer to the line camp. And it also explained why the mention of Trask's name had given Jerome a second's pause.

"Well," said Spencer, "I guess I understand what Al meant when he said we'd be short-handed around here. I'm supposed to go back up and fin-ish the work at the Bates place by myself."

Waltman twisted his mouth. "Work's work," he said.

"I left my bed up there," Spencer went on. "I suppose I can get a couple of blankets for tonight."

"There's some around," said Waltman.

Kern had taken out his jackknife and was cleaning his fingernails, but Galloway sat on the edge of his chair, tense, and his eyes went back and forth as he followed the conversation. Then he spoke.

"New coat?"

"The other one got ruined."

"Oh. Uh-huh."

Spencer took off the sheepskin and went over to lay it on his empty bunk. With the toe of his boot he nudged his valise, which he kept stowed beneath the bed. Then he returned to the company of the other three men and their silence.

"Any other news?" he asked.

"I'd think that's enough," said Waltman. "You get the kid killed, and Al fires a rustler." He lifted his head in an insolent way that reminded Spencer of Trask's nickname for Waltman: High Hat.

"You sound kind of free with that term," said Spencer.

"Why not? A man carries a runnin' iron, that's what he gets called."

"Behind his back."

Waltman sat straight up. "Well, well."

"I'll tell you," said Spencer. "It's like callin' a man a liar, or a horse thief, or what you will. You say something like that, you'd better be ready to back it up. Of course, once he's gone, it's easier."

Waltman held up his large head and kept his mouth closed even though his jaw was lowered. It was his pose of authority. "Well, I'll tell you," he mimicked. "You've got a lot of room to talk."

"No more than you," Spencer cut in. "Or any of us four. We all mavericked through the winter, but no one ever says anything about that. It's all right if you do it for your boss, and he's got plenty of friends in the Association."

Waltman's eyes narrowed. "It's not what I was gettin' to."

"I wouldn't think so."

"What I was gettin' to is, you seem to make friends with men that when their name comes up, that word does, too."

"It's a handy way of puttin' a smear on someone's name, I'd say. Is that what you're trying to do with me?"

Waltman sneered. "No one has to try with you, not when you do it yourself. You get friendly with rustlers, and people who have much to do with you get a dose of bad luck. You're makin' a name for yourself just fine, between that and your social calls."

Spencer's face tensed. "Sounds like you're ready to do your part to make sure that reputation gets passed around."

"Like I told you, I don't have to do anything. Just let you go on as you've been doin'—make friends here, pick up dead men there."

Spencer cut in again. "You make pretty light of it. I don't think you would if you were in my place. Maybe you think Perk's gonna walk through that door, but I was there, and I know that what happened is real, and it was no small thing."

"If I was in your place," said Waltman, in his mocking tone. "Well, I wasn't, and I'm not."

"I was sent up there, just like the time before. I didn't choose what happened either time."

Waltman's answer was quick. "You chose to get off track."

"When?" Spencer had the fleeting thought that someone had observed him and Perk take their detour to the road ranch.

"When Cliff Ardmore was killed."

Spencer felt as if he had dropped his guard and let a punch come through. "My whereabouts are accounted for on that day," he said.

"Sure. Just like I've been sayin'. You were makin' a name for yourself, over there sniffin' after the rustler's widow."

Spencer's temper flared, but he had the presence of mind not to lay into Waltman. Instead, he took in the little scene around the stove, which had fallen into uncomfortable silence after Waltman's words.

Kern, with his head bent, had his attention fixed on his jackknife and fingernails. Galloway sat with his right leg and stovepipe boot hooked over his left leg. His hands were folded together on his raised thigh, and his birdlike head was turned toward Spencer. Waltman, meanwhile, sat erect with his bulletlike head poking up from his neck and shoulders, as if he were waiting for someone to answer his challenge.

Spencer broke the silence. "I thought it was a point of decency not to mention a woman directly in conversation like this. I got called on it myself, and as I recall, you were listening."

"That was different."

Spencer tried to keep himself calm in the face of what seemed like a slur. "I'll give you a chance to take it back, Dick."

"You'll give me a chance? Oh, go peddle your papers, boy."

"I mean it."

Waltman ran the tip of his tongue along the inside of his lower lip. "And what if I don't accept the chance you're offerin' me?"

"That's your choice. But I imagine I'll have to ask you to step outside if you can't do the simple decent thing that's expected."

Kern's and Galloway's heads moved together as they looked at Spencer and then at Waltman.

"You make me laugh," said the big man. "But if you want to go outside, I'll oblige you."

"I guess that's it, then." Spencer moved to his bunk, where he took off his hat and tossed it on top of the sheepskin coat. Then he took off his gun and holster and set them on the bed as well. There was no turning back at this point.

Waltman stood waiting by the rear door, which was now open. Spencer could see daylight still showing outside. He supposed it was better that way, not having to peer and grope in the darkness. He walked to the doorway, paying no attention to Waltman, and was stepping over the threshold when he felt a hard shove in his back. He stumbled out and landed on his knees on the damp ground. When he came up and around, Waltman was closing in on him.

A roundhouse blow to his left cheekbone set him staggering back. Then Waltman hooked with his left and caught Spencer on the right temple. The big man came straight ahead, throwing a right punch that glanced off Spencer's upraised forearms. Spencer connected once, landing his right fist on Waltman's cheek.

The big man stepped back, then came forward again. He threw four or five punches in succession, skidding off Spencer's guard and once off the top of his head. Spencer swung but could not connect. Waltman had too much reach on him.

Spencer dropped back and moved to his left, bounced in to throw a jab, and met with a fist in the teeth. A second blow to the temple rocked him, and then a roundhouse on his left ear sent him sprawling backward onto the muddy ground.

He rolled over and came up, hoping Waltman could not hit him hard enough to knock him out. He raised his guard and waited for the next series of punches, hoping to find an opening. Instead, he felt Waltman's grip come clamping down onto his wrists, and the big man swung him to one side and threw him onto the ground again. As Spencer came up to his knees, a swinging boot to his left side knocked him into the cold mud one more time.

He got his feet under him and pushed himself upward into a crouch. Then he had his guard up and was trying to fend off blows, trying to keep moving, trying to keep from getting knocked down again.

But it happened anyway. Waltman hammered at his forearms, at his upper arms and shoulders, at his ribs. Then a fist out of nowhere caught him on the left cheekbone and knocked him down.

A ringing, buzzing sensation surrounded his head as he rolled onto all fours and waited. He did not like the feeling of hoping it was over, hoping the big man would not hit him anymore. He knew that was what he was doing, asking for quarter. It shamed him, for he knew he had lost after calling out the other man.

Waltman stood over him, looming. "Had enough?"

"I suppose so." Spencer made himself look up.

"Well, I hope you remember it." Waltman turned and cast an imperious glance at his audience, which consisted of Kern and Galloway a couple of paces from the back step, plus Mac the cook staring out from the doorway.

Mac turned away and disappeared inside. Kern and Galloway let Waltman go first, and then they followed him into the bunkhouse.

Spencer rose to his feet and took a couple of deep breaths. He didn't feel very steady, and his head seemed disconnected, but at least he hadn't been knocked out. As he took stock of himself, he saw that his shirt was smeared and smudged, worse than his trousers, from the various times he had hit the ground, plus the contact from Waltman's boot. His eyes felt as if they wanted to close, but he held them open as he leaned over, hands on his knees, and took more deep breaths.

He straightened up and brushed off what dirt he could. Again he had to open his eyes and make an effort to hold them that way. Noting the dim light, he reminded himself that it was late afternoon, not morning, that he hadn't just awakened but rather had been knocked on the side of the head one too many times. He took another deep breath, pulled himself together, and walked to the door of the bunkhouse.

Waltman was seated at the table with his back to the door, so Spencer did not have to look at him. Kern and Galloway, on the other side of the table, kept their eyes averted. Spencer stepped inside, steadied himself, and walked to his bunk. At first he thought he would dig out a clean shirt and put it on, but when he pulled the valise from under the bed, he decided he would leave now instead of in the morning. He would take his clean clothes with him and change somewhere along the way. He didn't know where. His mind was too clouded. But he knew he didn't want to stay at the bunkhouse.

He set the valise on the bed and laid the sheepskin coat over it. After slipping his holster and pistol back onto his belt and putting on his hat, he tucked the coat and valise in the crook of his arm and left through the open back door. Outside he waited for a long moment, letting his head clear some more. He heard footsteps in front of the bunkhouse, then the opening and closing of a door. From the tone of voices, he gathered that Al Jerome had gone in for the evening meal.

Spencer stood in the cool of the evening for another moment, gathering his senses. It was a long ways to the line camp, and he didn't want to be rummy when he got there, but he had to get out of this place. Things didn't add up right, and he needed to sort them out.

He went to the horse corral and looked at his choices. Even though the dark horse never seemed to tire, he had just ridden it all the way north and back, and furthermore he didn't want to be riding something that might spook in the night, especially when he was a bit light-headed. He settled on the stocky sorrel, which he knew was a good night horse and also had good wind.

He saddled the horse, tied the valise on back with the bundle in the slicker, and led the horse out into the yard. For a moment, a daze fell upon him, a dull cloud that made him narrow his eyes. He studied the saddle to make sure it was his, then told himself it couldn't be anyone else's if it had his slicker tied on back. Things seemed normal again, for the moment. He grabbed the saddle horn, boosted, and swung his leg up and over. Dusk was gathering as he rode out of the ranch yard of the A-J.

By the time he got to the fork in the road south of the buttes, some two hours later, his head had cleared enough for him to decide to spend the night in town instead of riding all the way to the line camp in the dark. He could put the horse in a stable, and for another two bits he could sleep in the straw. That sounded like a good plan. He turned the sorrel to the right fork and rode through the buttes as the moon rose in the night sky.

In the stable, he tended to his things by lantern light. He spread Perkins's denim coat out on a stanchion to let it dry, and he laid his slicker on the straw. With the slicker as his ground sheet and the horse blanket over him, he would have enough of a bed to sleep in for one night.

Sitting in the straw, he pulled the valise over and unbuckled the two straps. He knew he had a clean shirt in there, and he wanted to check on socks. But when he took out the shirt, he saw something he would never have expected. It was a Colt .45 pistol with ivory grips, silent and deadly and bare.

Things still didn't add up in a perfect column, but they began to make sense. He couldn't know it for certain, but it sure seemed as if Al Jerome had sent him up to the Bates place the first time so his return would coincide with Cliff Ardmore's death. Then the second trip was supposed to be the end of Spencer, after which the discovery of Ardmore's pistol would fix the blame on him. It would look as if he was shot for being one of Jerome's men, and then when he was not around to speak for himself, it would come out that he was a traitor after all. No wonder Jerome was so surprised to see him. He was expecting Perkins, and he had sent Trask on his way so there would be fewer people to ask questions.

Spencer set the pistol back in the valise and covered it with the shirt. The way he had just figured things out made sense, but he reminded himself that there might be other explanations. And even if his hunch about Jerome was right, he didn't have an idea of why Jerome would have his cohort with the ivory-handled pistol done in.

Then there were other things to consider, such as how much Waltman knew. If Jerome had hired someone to go to the Bates place and shoot a man, Waltman might or might not be aware of it. The same went for Ardmore's death and the telltale pistol. Spencer found it easy to imagine Waltman planting the gun in the valise, yet anyone could have done it. It was hard to tell how deep Waltman was in on things, but the more he knew, the more danger he posed to Spencer. A drubbing with the fists seemed like small stakes compared to the rest.

Spencer came back to the moment. It would not take long for someone at the A-J headquarters— whoever had planted the pistol—to see that the valise was gone. The person would know that Spencer knew someone had made a move against him. So the cat was out of the bag in that respect. For Spencer there was no riding back into the A-J, taking his place at the table, and acting as if nothing had happened. To the contrary, he was going to have to try to keep a step ahead of Al Jerome.

Chapter Eleven

Spencer did not blow out the light and go to sleep. All the way into town he thought he would be able to fall asleep as soon as he lay down, but with the discovery of the pistol in his valise, he had come wide awake. His mind had started to click, and he did not want to lie down. As he sat in the straw, he felt a restlessness all through his body and down to his legs. He wanted to get up and around, do something. If he was going to spend a night in town, he needed to take some kind of action rather than just hole up. It wasn't that late yet—between ten and eleven, he figured—and he had a feeling he might learn something or see someone if he went out and took a look around.

The nagging grew within him. He had to do something. He had told Eva he would, and he had made a pledge to Perkins. So far, all he had accomplished was the fight with Waltman, which had left him in a near stupor. Now he was awake, wondering about a dozen different unanswered questions. If he could get even the hint of an answer to one of them, he would be getting somewhere.

One question that came up, like a swimmer to the surface of a pond or a figure emerging from the fog, took the shape of a compact, dark-featured man with a full mustache and quick, dark eyes. A brown hat with an upturned brim. A dark neckerchief and a brown wool vest. Where was Trask? Spencer had no doubt that the running iron was a setup, especially in light of the planted pistol. He figured Trask would have taken good warning, but he didn't have a clear hunch as to whether the man would have hit the trail for better places or whether he might have hung around to compare impressions with Spencer. If he had stayed around, he might be in town this evening.

Now that Spencer had the idea that Trask might be in the vicinity, it seemed as if he should be. He might be standing in the Rawhide Saloon at this very moment, taking small sips of his drink and watching who came and went.

Spencer took the clean shirt out of the valise again, pulled off the one that had gotten dirty in the fight with Waltman, and put on the clean one. He stuffed the dirty shirt in the bag, covering the pistol and enclosing it. Then he pushed the valise into the straw and covered it with his slicker.

Standing up, he tucked in the shirt and put on his sheepskin coat. His mind was clear now, and he had no intention of clouding it up with too many drinks. Just one would do—something to give justification for standing in the saloon.

He blew out the kerosene lamp, and from the light of another just like it at the other end of the stable, he found his way to the door and out into the chilly night.

The town lay quiet under a clear, quarter-moon sky. Spencer didn't see anyone out on the sidewalks, and only a couple of horses stood hipshot in front of the Rawhide. The barbershop sat in darkness, and Spencer imagined Perkins was lying in a pine box in the back room. If Trask was in town, he would have heard the news about the kid and would be on the lookout for Spencer.

Inside the Rawhide Saloon, the lantern light was neither dim nor bright. A haze of tobacco smoke hung in the air, and the level of talk was calm. No one paid Spencer much attention as he closed the door behind him and made his way to the bar.

Rex of the eyeglasses and disappearing chin stood with his hands resting with his light touch on the bar top.

"Yes, sir?" he asked.

"Just a glass of whiskey."

Rex nodded and pushed away, and with a few small motions he set up a glass, poured the drink, and corked the bottle.

Spencer took out a silver dollar, but before letting go of it he asked the barkeep, "You remember that fellow named Trask who came in here with me a few times?"

"Not the kid? I heard he got killed."

"No, not him. The other one. Medium-sized, dark hair and whiskers."

"Oh, sure. I remember him. Serious type. Doesn't say much."

"That's him. You haven't seen him in the last day or so, have you?"

Rex shook his head. "No, not at all."

Spencer pushed the silver dollar across the bar top.

Rex furrowed his brow and spoke again. "I thought you worked with him."

"I did, but he left the ranch when I was gone, and I was just wondering if he was still around."

Rex shrugged, then took the coin and turned away.

Spencer took a sip of his whiskey and let his eyes travel around the barroom. Nothing extraordinary came to his attention, as eight or nine men were scattered along the bar to his left. The only patron Spencer recognized except in a vague, distant way was the jug-eared teamster who had slapped Perkins on the shoulder one night. Turning to his right, Spencer saw that the place at the end of the bar near the deer antlers was unoccupied, and he expected Robinson the lawyer to walk in any minute.

Time dragged on without the man's appearance, though. No one came or left, and the mutter of conversation stayed the same. Then, as Spencer cast another thoughtless glance toward the right end of the bar, he felt a jolt at the sight of a familiar figure. There in his customary place stood Wolf Carlton, aloof and self-assured as always.

Spencer noted the dark hat with the ridged crown, the dark wool coat and vest, the large round eyes, and the prominent cheekbones, then the trimmed mustache, the narrow jaws and chin, and the peaked ears. Spencer's heartbeat had picked up with his initial recognition, and it chilled him to wonder whether Carlton had drawn a bead on the tan canvas coat. Whether Carlton had done that piece of work or not, he had a willingness to do the dirty work for men like Al Jerome. For that, Spencer found it in himself to despise the stock detective. He was a man who could kill someone he had nothing against, either in principle or on a personal level. If he made a mistake and killed the wrong person, as might have been the case with Perkins, he would not allow himself to see it as a personal wrong. It was just a mistake, which he could try to rectify by getting the right man the next time.

The chill crept across Spencer's neck and shoulders as he realized that Carlton not only might have been out to kill him but might yet do it. If that was what Carlton was up to, he would know that Spencer had a strong hunch that the bullet aimed at the tan coat had been intended for him.

But if Carlton had any such ideas, he did not show it. He kept to his corner and minded his own business, and if he was stealing glances at a man he planned to kill, it was probably not the first time he had done such a thing. None of it was personal, and he had to be confident that things would go his way next time. In his business, he could not doubt himself, not any more than he could question a course of action.

Spencer took a drink to steady himself. It was unnerving to think that twenty-five feet away stood a man who indeed might kill him, yet it gave him an opportunity for caution that Perk never had. For one thing, Wolf Carlton was not going to kill him tonight, and for another, he was not going to have as easy pickin's as he might have had on some other occasion.

Now the stock detective tossed off the rest of his drink. As was his habit, he walked around the corner of the bar and made a lingering turn to the front door. As he did so, Spencer was sure the man took a full look at the sheepskin coat and verified who was wearing it. Carlton did not take the chill with him as he walked out the front door into the night.

Spencer stayed for a second drink. He knew that even if Carlton had him on his list, the man wouldn't try anything in town. He would wait until he thought he had everything under control in some remote place. All the same, Spencer waited until a group of three men left, and he went out a few steps behind them. As they mounted up and went on their way, he walked the three blocks to the livery stable. Once there, he found his bed in the dark and turned in.

Morning came with dim light, the sound of horses shuffling and the stable man talking to them, the clean smell of straw, and the warm smell of horses. As Spencer shifted in bed, he felt sore and stiff from the fight the evening before. He was also hungry.

Still huddled under the blanket, he decided to go out for breakfast before getting his horse ready for the day's work. He rolled out of bed and pulled on his boots, then put on his hat and coat and went out into the chilly gray morning.

The smell of wood smoke drifted on the thin air as Spencer turned into the main street and looked up and down the blank thoroughfare. The Durham Café was open, casting pale lamplight through the window out onto the sidewalk. As Spencer went inside, two men in range clothes looked up with incurious eyes and went back to

eating. The smell of fried food sparked his appe-
tite even more than before, and he took a seat by
himself at the counter, where he thought the food
might arrive quicker. A drab-looking biscuit-
shooter poured him a cup of coffee and took his
order of fried potatoes, ham, and flapjacks. Before he finished his first cup of coffee, his meal
arrived. From where he sat he had a view of the
front door, so he gave a sideways glance now and
then as he put away the food.

Back out on the street, he felt watched. He did
not see anyone, and most of the windows were
still dark. He wondered if the feeling came from
his sense of being conspicuous in the new sheepskin coat. He still assumed that no one would
make a play for him in town, yet he felt like a
walking target.

He did not go straight to the livery stable but
rather went around three blocks and came in
through the back way. Once inside, having settled with the stable man, Spencer decided how to
pack his gear. He saddled the stocky sorrel, then
tied on the leather gripsack. Next he rolled up the
sheepskin coat in his slicker and tied the bundle
on top of the valise. Perk's denim coat was still
damp, but Spencer braced himself and put it on.
He tucked his own hat inside the coat, pulled
Perk's large, dark hat low onto his brow, and led
the horse outside. He checked the cinch, set his
reins, got his boot in the stirrup, swung his leg up
and over, and settled into the cold saddle.

He rode east for a block, south for two, and back
west. At the edge of town he set out southwest
across the open country. He supposed that Wolf

Carlton would expect him to go north, or west and then north, to return to the line camp. Sooner or later he would go there, but for the time being he thought he would go in an unexpected direction, neither toward the Bates place nor back toward the A-J. On second thought, maybe no direction he took was unexpected, especially since he had a reason for going where he was now headed.

A strong smell of smoke came on a breeze as he topped the last little rise coming into the Wingate homestead. It took him an instant to realize that a blank spot in the picture coincided with a black heap of smoking ruins where the stable had once stood. Then he matched the thick odor with the smoldering remains.

Eva's little bay horse and the sorrel with white socks in front stood hunched to the wind, looking out over the top rail of the corral. With the overcast morning and the sharp edge on the wind, the scene gave a bleak feeling.

The footfalls of Spencer's horse sounded hollow as he rode into the yard. He had put on his own hat a few minutes earlier, and he held his head up as he faced the house.

The front door opened a crack, then a little more as Eva Wingate came into view. She was wearing a work shirt and trousers, and her hair hung loose to her shoulders. Even at thirty yards, the tenseness on her face was visible.

He brought his horse to a stop at the hitching rail and swung down.

"Go ahead and tie him, and come on in," she said. "That wind's a little chilly."

He tied up the sorrel, left Perk's hat on the saddle horn, and walked to the front door. Eva stepped back and let him in. As he crossed the threshold, he saw a rifle leaning against the door-jamb on his left.

She closed the door and turned, lifting her blue eyes to meet him. "Things aren't getting any better," she said.

"It doesn't look like it. Did someone try to burn you out?"

"Seems that way. They set fire to the stable, opened the corral, and scattered the horses. The two you saw, they came back, but I don't have a plan yet for how to find the others."

"When did this happen?"

"Yesterday morning. Just before dawn. I heard some commotion, horses getting stirred up, and then I heard them running off. I thought I heard a crackling sound, and when I went to the door, I saw the stable was on fire. There wasn't much I could do except watch it burn."

The odor of burned materials, heavier than the clean smell of wood smoke, hung in his nostrils. "Did you lose all your tools and gear?"

She gave a solemn nod. "Pretty much. I had my saddle here in the house, where I was cleaning it, along with my bridle, but everything else is gone. The other saddle, various ropes and harness, even those burlap bags I worked on."

He shook his head. "That's a dirty way to do things. You say it happened yesterday morning?"

"That's right."

"They're movin' pretty fast, then."

Her blue eyes flashed. "Why do you say that?"

"At about that same time, someone fired a shot at a line camp up north where I was stayin'. I'm pretty sure it was intended for me, but it got this young kid Perkins instead. When I went back to the ranch headquarters, I found out my other pal, Trask, the one who was riding with me the day we found Collins, got fired while I was gone."

Her eyes searched him. "What do you think it means?"

"I don't know. Seems like they're makin' a clean sweep, or tryin' to. Get me and Trask out of the way, and try to push you out. What do you think?"

"Well, I had no idea of anything else that was going on, but I sure felt I was being pushed." She paused as her eyes roved. "Why do you think they would want to make a move against you?"

At this point he remembered to take off his hat, so he did. "Well," he said, "a variety of things, I guess. To begin with, they didn't like my bein' friends with you folks. The boss told me that much outright. As time went on, I suppose he liked it less, didn't want us to be comparin' what we knew. Then, I think they wanted to make it look like I was the one who did in Cliff Ardmore, and if I wasn't around to speak up for myself, they could hang it on me easier."

"Really?" she said, with a quick intake of breath. "Whoever 'they' is, I thought it included Mr. Ardmore, rather than someone who had it in for him."

"I did, too, and it may have, at one time. But I think something changed, maybe without his knowing it until it was too late. The sheriff seems to think, or maybe finds it convenient to think,

that the whole thing's a feud with one bunch goin'
tit for tat, as he put it, against the other."

Eva frowned.

"I know. It doesn't make sense. As far as I know,
there's no association of little operators. What few
are left won't stick together even if one of 'em
wanted to. You've told me that."

She shook her head. "No, it doesn't make sense."

Spencer continued. "They try to paint me as a fellow who sympathizes with this bunch that really
doesn't exist. The sheriff and Jerome both put it that
way when Ardmore came to grief. Then they turn
around and say that whoever shot Perk was gettin'
even with the big cattlemen and got one of their
men. But Perk was wearin' my coat. I'm convinced
that whoever shot him was after me, so if someone
believes this whole rustler story, that there's a band
of small-timers and I sympathize with 'em, then the
follow-up is that they went way out of their way to
try to rub out one of their allies. It just goes around
in a circle and makes no sense at all."

Eva narrowed her eyes. "So which side are you
supposed to be on, according to this story?"

"That's just it. I'm on whatever side they can get
someone to believe. And I think 'they' is mostly
Al Jerome. I was puzzled by Cliff Ardmore gettin' killed—excuse me for putting it so bluntly—
and it threw the whole thing out of balance. Jerome started acting as if someone had made a
move against him and his friends, but I couldn't
imagine who would do it. But then I saw where
the Ardmore business might have come from the
same source as what happened to George Farrow
and then Collins."

She frowned again. "What helped you see that?"

He hesitated, unsure how much to tell her. "When Cliff Ardmore came to the end of his luck, his pistol turned up missing. You might have noticed it, an ivory-handled thing he seemed proud of."

"Oh, yes. I remember that. He did seem a little vain about it."

"He did. Anyway, someone took it, and the natural thing was to assume it was the person who did him in. Makes sense. But then, after all this time, yesterday it showed up in my satchel, right there in the bunkhouse of the A-J."

Now she looked close at him. "Someone put it there?"

"That's right. I don't know whether Al Jerome planted it or whether he had one of his men do it, but it tells me a few things. One, Al Jerome was in on Ardmore's death. Two, he wanted to frame me for it. Three, he didn't think I'd live to find out. And four, he sent Trask on his way so he wouldn't poke around and ask questions about strange doin's."

She shook her head in puzzlement. "How could they 'frame' you, as you put it?"

"Well, it seems as if it might have all been set up. Al Jerome sent me up north on a job that would have me coming back through at about the time and place that someone got to Ardmore. But as it turned out, I had come around this way, and I was nowhere near there. But if I was out of the way when they found the pistol in my bag, they could twist things around to make it look like I could have done it anyway."

Her blue eyes seemed to be gazing beyond him. "Even at that," she said, "why would you have wanted to? Just because you were friends with Collins?"

Again he felt the uneasiness about how much to tell her. "Well, there was the little matter of my having gone to Ardmore's place to deliver a letter one day, and I ended up in a, um—well, it didn't look good."

"Oh, that," she said.

He thought she said it with a tone of dismissal, but he wasn't sure. He continued by saying, "It was a mistake on my part, I'll admit that. Things got flirtatious for a minute or two, nothin' more than that, but it didn't leave me lookin' very good. And for all I know, that was a setup, too, at least on Jerome's part. But whatever the case, it was my error, and I've felt stupid about it. Then when her husband died and that little incident was brought up against me, I felt even stupider."

"Well," said Eva, "as far as that part goes, you should try to put that behind you and concentrate on the present. It seems there's plenty to worry about there."

"Sure is," he said. "Like trying to keep from letting someone get me into his gun sights." Right away he added, "Sorry. That's a bit blunt, too, I guess."

Her face relaxed into a half smile. "You wear it well when you speak straight out like that," she said. "And it's not as if I'm too delicate to know or hear of such matters. After all, a couple of things have happened here."

"Oh, I know," he answered. "And I'm sorry. All I've done is talk about myself, and here you are, you've had someone try to burn you out. That can't go easy on you."

She spoke in a calm voice. "In comparison with what went before, having my stable burned is on a lesser scale. I can't know whether I've passed through the biggest crisis of my life, but this present one does not have me shaken to the roots. On the other hand, if it's part of an organized effort, as it seems to be, there's reason to expect more." She gave Spencer a close look. "This might be an easy thing to say, but I think they're just trying to scare me. I think that if I just sit tight, they won't try to burn me out all the way, or do actual harm to me."

"Maybe not. But you want to remember that some of these same kind of respectable cattlemen did hang a woman over on the Sweetwater. Of course they had their pretenses that she was some kind of a rustler or receiver of stolen cattle, but nevertheless that's what they did, and in the end they got away with it clean."

"I know that," said Eva. "But what I was getting around to saying was that there's less to worry about in my case than there is in yours. Whoever is behind this is clearly not done yet. But I don't want you to worry about me when you've got so much more looking out to do on your own behalf. Like I say, I can sit tight for a while at least."

"I imagine you can," he conceded. "But like you also said, they're not done. If you don't pack up and leave—which I gather you don't want to do, and I'd be sorry to see you do it as well—they'll come back and try something else."

Her eyes came to his. "You think Al Jerome is behind this, too, then?"

"It all seems to fit. As for the actual deed, he would have someone else do that while he and his boys had a perfect alibi. And as for who actually set the match, that could be someone we've never seen before. I assume you didn't get a glimpse of anyone."

She shook her head. "No, not at all."

After a couple of seconds, Spencer went on. "You know, there's this fellow named Wolf Carlton around."

"I remember that name well enough. Collins mentioned it a few times, and I think I referred to it once with you."

"You did." After a pause, Spencer said, "I think he's Al Jerome's triggerman. But I don't think he would bother with firin' someone's barn. I mention him, though, because he seems to get around pretty well, and I think he's as dangerous as he can be." Spencer let his eyes meet hers. "It's hard to just come out and accuse him when you've got no proof. But if anything happens to me, I sure hope someone looks into his whereabouts at the time."

Her gaze was steady and serious. "You think he's the one who killed Collins, then."

"Collins, George Farrow, and this kid Perkins, they all fit his style. Dry-gulch 'em. On the other hand, he could very well be the one who got Cliff Ardmore, too. If he was on terms with Jerome and Ardmore's little syndicate, he could ride right up to the man and put him away."

"And take his pistol."

"Sure."

Eva brushed back a wisp of her dark hair. "What do you think you can do, then?"

"Well, first off, I have to keep from getting shot.

That means I have to stay on the dodge until I can get something to go to the law with."

"If no one's been able to do that yet, how are you going to?"

"I'm not sure. For one thing, our good sheriff seems to lean toward Al Jerome, and for all I know, he's afraid of Wolf Carlton. At any rate, no one has scratched very deep. If I could get something convincing, I might be able to swing the pendulum the other way."

She gave him a questioning look. "But you have no idea how you might do that?"

He paused. "Well, I wouldn't say I've got no idea. I've got one, and I don't know how good it is."

Her face relaxed into a sympathetic expression. "Oh, well, if it's something you think you'd rather not say out loud, I don't mean to—"

"No, not at all. I just don't know if it would do any good—or worse, if it would do some harm."

She gave a light shrug.

"My idea is that I could try asking someone I'm not sure of. I think there's one person who might be able to tell me something about why Al Jerome would turn on one of his own kind."

Eva frowned. "And who would that be?"

"Mrs. Ardmore."

Eva let out an audible breath, and her eyes opened. "Who knows?" she said. "You might learn something."

"I think I've got a better chance there than trying to get anything out of the three hired hands left at the A-J." He paused for a couple of seconds, twisting the corner of his mouth. "Thing is, I'm not sure how to approach her. I don't even know how reasonable it would be to ride up to the ranch house."

"Oh, as far as that goes, I understand she's moved into town, taken a room at the Paragon Hotel."

Spencer raised his eyebrows. "That's better than I thought. I don't feel that I have to worry about getting sniped at in town. And if she decides she doesn't want to talk to me, I can be out of there in a minute, back on the street. No long ride back and forth, wonderin' if anyone's waitin' for me." He paused again. "Of course, I still have to consider what it might look like."

"Pah," said Eva. "I would hope you don't worry about that, when there's so much else at stake. I sure wouldn't."

Spencer smiled. "That's good to know."

"As if my opinion mattered."

"Well, it does," he said. "You're the one person I feel I can trust in all of this."

She gave him a look that was almost admonishing. "I certainly hope you can." Then she added, "I also hope your visit goes all right. And I think it's good you're taking some initiative and not just staying on the dodge, as you say."

"Oh, I know that."

Silence hung in the air for several seconds until she said, "Well, if and when something changes, I hope you let me know about it."

"I hope I'm able to."

She put out her hand. "Good luck, Spencer."

"Thank you, ma'am." He tipped her a nod.

She shook her head in a little tease. "If I'm going to call you by your name, as you asked me to before, you can call me by mine."

"Good enough, Eva. I hope I make it back with a good report."

"So do I."

The shine of her eyes and the half smile that played on her face stayed with him as he left her house, mounted up, and rode out of the ranch yard.

Chapter Twelve

The sorrel horse didn't seem to want to settle down. He kept snuffling and throwing his head and bunching up like he wanted to run. Spencer wondered what had gotten into the horse, whether it was the clogging smoke from the day-old smoldering ruins or the chilly wind with the threat of colder weather coming up. Whatever it was, the horse wouldn't even out. Spencer loped him for about half a mile, but the sorrel kept crow-hopping and wanting to break into a dead run. Spencer didn't want to give him his head, so he reined him in again. The sorrel went back to snorting, shaking the bridle, and sidestepping. Spencer made him go in a circle, then a hundred yards later made him do it again, but still the horse did not calm down.

Meanwhile, Spencer had not been following a planned course. When he left the Wingate place, he rode southwest through the rolling grassland, following an easy trail that he remembered from the day he and Trask had brought in Collins Wingate. When the trail opened into broader country, Spencer concentrated more on staying in the saddle and trying to keep the sorrel horse under control than on plotting his course.

The sun had risen in the sky and had passed mid-morning, but it was pale in the thin cloud cover, and the breeze out of the west kept the air chilly. Spencer had the denim coat buttoned all the way up with Perk's hat stuffed inside. He thought it would be a good idea to change hats, but he didn't want to be fiddling around and getting his hands distracted if the horse took a notion to bolt. So he rode along, more or less southwest, uncertain whether he wanted to hook around to the west or to the east.

Figuring the time of day, and remembering that he had left two horses in the corral at the line camp, he decided to go east and see about dropping into town on his way to tend to the horses. He put the sorrel into a circle again, then reined him out of it and headed east. With the breeze at his rump, the horse seemed to settle down a little, but still he threw his head, shook the bit, and quick-stepped. Spencer pulled his hat down snug and rode on. He recognized the broad area where he and Trask and Waltman had found Wingate's body, but the grassland showed no trace of anything ever having happened there.

Within a quarter of an hour he was into rolling country again, and he divided his attention between keeping the horse under control and studying the land forms around him. Wolf Carlton could be anywhere, and for all Spencer knew, the man could have been following him on his circuitous route this morning and might even have gotten out on the trail ahead of him.

The sorrel continued to fidget, and Spencer was beginning to wonder if he should dismount and check his rigging. He recalled how the horse had kept stepping away when he had tried to swing aboard in the Wingate ranch yard, and he didn't want to go through that difficulty again out on the open prairie. He was weighing one precaution against another when without warning the sorrel stopped and whinnied.

Spencer looked up and around, and his upper body tensed as he recognized the horseman. He was a big man on a tall chestnut gelding that Spencer knew right away. The rider wore his customary high-crowned hat, round on top like a bullet head, and he also had on a dark wool coat that emphasized his bulk.

As Waltman came closer, Spencer noted the man's leather riding gloves, his saddle with the high swells and cantle and full, square skirts, and then the rifle and scabbard by his left knee. Waltman held his chin up as the glossy chestnut came stepping forward. When he was within ten yards, his coarse voice sounded on the thin air.

"You look like you're lost, boy."

"Not much."

Waltman's rough complexion and full face made his eyes seem narrow as they took in Spencer and his outfit. "You ought to have been up at that line camp by now," he said, "but it looks as if you're on the move."

"Is that where you want me, up at the line camp?"

Waltman relaxed his eyes. "It's where you're supposed to be, if you're workin' for the A-J and ridin' company horses."

"I'm takin' the long way around."

"Too long, I'd say."

Spencer observed the man's heavy features—
the large nose, thick ears and neck—and wished
he had landed a few more punches the evening
before. Then he remarked, "I'd wonder why your
say matters. Did you get promoted to foreman?"

Waltman's face tensed. "I don't need smart comments from you, and you'd just as well know that
Al told me to keep an eye out for you, just in case
you spent the night at Widda Wingate's instead of
goin' to your job like you're supposed to."

Spencer burned, but he made himself hold steady.
"Is that what you do best—spy on other people?"

Waltman raised his unshaven chin again in a
pose of arrogance as he said, "I thought I gave you
a sample yesterday of what I do well."

"Maybe you did. Maybe more than you want to."

The eyes narrowed. "What do you mean by
that?"

Spencer thought he might have struck a nerve
about the ivory-handled pistol, as Waltman had
seen the leather satchel; but rather than tip his
hand there, Spencer said, "I thought maybe you
were handy at settin' a match."

Waltman cocked his head and squinted his left
eye. "I don't have the slightest idea what you
mean, boy, but I don't like the sound of it."

Spencer shrugged. "Well, if you don't know anything about it, I won't trouble you with details."

"You might have to tell someone about details,"
said the big man. With a sneer he added, "Explain
where you've been when you're supposed to be
workin'."

"Maybe I am working."

"Don't look like it."

"I'll tell you, it's hard work just puttin' up with you."

Waltman stiffened. "You've got a lot of smart talk for someone in your position."

Something lit up in Spencer's mind, but he wasn't sure what it was. "Is that right?" he said. "What position would that be?"

Waltman's smug look had returned. "Don't know, huh? Well, I'll tell ya, and I think you know it pretty damn well already." Waltman wrinkled his nose. "It has to do with the friends you make."

"I choose my own friends, in spite of your wise counsel. But what position does that put me in?"

"As if you didn't know. But I'll tell you flat out. You've gotten yourself quite a reputation for sidin' with rustlers."

Spencer cut in. "That is, accordin' to people who toss that word around so easy."

Waltman went on, ignoring the comment. "And with that reputation, you've given out two reasons for makin' a move against Cliff Ardmore."

"Two, you say?"

"Count 'em. Rustler sympathy, and a little bit of jealousy."

"Oh, hell, that's trumped up. I never so much as touched that woman."

Waltman gave a wide, downturned smile that spread his face out. "Oh, I didn't mean her, though you thought of it quick enough. I meant your little widda friend over this way. Everyone knows that Cliff was slippin' by to see her, and you was spyin' on him and not likin' it."

Things began to add up fast. Spencer said, "It doesn't surprise me that Wolf Carlton reports to Jerome, then."

Waltman shrugged. "Oh, if he saw you, too, that's another matter. Like I said, everyone knows it."

"Everyone."

"Sure, just like everyone knows what a pal you were to Wingate and that quaky fella that rode for George Farrow. Rustler pal, jealous about your rustler gal." Waltman's glance strayed toward the back of Spencer's saddle until he brought his eyes back to bear on Spencer himself.

"You talk as if you speak for a big majority, Dick, but I think 'everyone' in your story is you, Al Jerome, and maybe the sheriff. But I'll tell you this. You know damn well I'm not a rustler or a killer, either one. You're just tryin' to paint me that way to cover up what someone else has done. It's as plain as the nose on your face."

Waltman's expression turned to stone. It was clear that he didn't like the reference to his nose, but it was also clear that he didn't like someone calling his hand. In a surly voice he said, "I don't like someone talking in a way that amounts to callin' me a liar."

Up until now, Spencer's horse had been calm in the presence of the chestnut, but when the bigger horse flinched, the sorrel did as well. When Spencer got the reins snugged, he saw that Waltman had brought out his six-gun and had it leveled across the swells of his saddle.

"Don't make this thing go off," he said, his voice gravelly as he cocked the gun. "It could happen."

Spencer looked at the muzzle of the .45 and saw it as something real and dangerous, not just a threat.

Waltman spoke again. "Thing is, little friend, enough people have their suspicions about you that you're goin' to have to answer some questions." He waved the gun. "I'm takin' you in for investigation."

"Ah, you can't do that. You're no lawman."

The man in the bullet-head hat waggled the .45 again and seemed to rise in the saddle with his tomcat assurance. "I don't need to be, as long as I've got this."

"Makes you big."

"Big enough. But it's not just me. You've got some answerin' to do." Waltman fingered the reins with his left hand. "Now let's have that gun," he said. "Put your right hand on the saddle horn, and reach across with your left. Hike up that coat, and lift out your gun by the handle. Don't get anywhere near the trigger, or this one might go off."

As Spencer passed the reins to his right hand, he felt the horse shift beneath him. He did not like the idea of reaching across with his left hand and putting himself off balance.

"Hold that horse still," said Waltman.

"He's been actin' up all morning."

"My ass. You're doin' somethin' to him, so quit it. Just pull out that gun and hold it at arm's length, pointing down."

"I'm not doing anything to him."

"Just shut up and reach across like I told you." Waltman waved the gun and then held it straight at Spencer.

With Perk's hat inside the buttoned coat, the reach was almost impossible. Spencer kept his right hand resting on the saddle horn and his elbow cocked up like a chicken wing. As he reached across, he had to twist in his seat, and just as his fingertips touched the butt of his pistol, the sorrel horse burst forward.

Spencer lost his right stirrup and popped up, back, and then forward. He clawed at the saddle horn with his right hand and at the reins with his left. A bullet tore the air next to him, and the crack of the pistol shot followed. The sorrel crow-hopped, and Spencer lost his left stirrup. The right rein was trailing. With his left hand he held the remaining rein and tried to grab a hank of the horse's mane. He had hold of the saddle horn, but he had bounced up from the saddle and had his right leg hung up on the bundle he had tied on in back. The horse crow-hopped again, and he slipped to his left. He hung way off balance, and his right leg was prying him up. He was sure he was going to hit head and shoulder on the hard ground streaming by beneath him, and he didn't know how to stay clear of the horse's hooves. If anything, his trailing leg would drag him underneath.

A second shot cracked through the air, and the horse jumped again with its hindquarters to the right. Spencer took a dive to the left, where he hit hard and rolled over once, then came to a halt as his forehead dug a small trench in the dirt. The horse thundered on.

Spencer came up on all fours, then stood and bent over with his hands on his knees. His left side throbbed and stung, but it did not feel as if anything was broken. He had forgotten about his pistol, Waltman, and everything else until he heard the other horse come jostling up behind him.

"That was stupid as hell," came Waltman's voice. "Now suppose we pick up where we left off, and you lift out that six-gun with your left hand."

With his left arm aching, Spencer did as he was told and handed the gun up to Waltman, who sat easy in the saddle with his .45 trained on Spencer.

"Now pick up your hat, and we'll go get that horse."

Spencer looked around and found where his hat had fallen and lay tipped against a clump of sagebrush. After dusting it off and settling it over his scratched forehead, he set out toward the horse. It stood about a hundred and fifty yards away at three-quarters profile, reins hanging to the ground as it kept a wide left eye on the man approaching on foot.

Waltman plodded behind on the chestnut. "Don't try anything foolish this time," he called out. "I might not miss again."

When Spencer came within twenty yards of the horse, it raised its head to one side and trotted away, reins trailing. A hundred yards away, it stopped and took up the same profile as before. Spencer walked toward it, and once again it took off when he came within twenty yards. Man and horse kept up the stop-and-go routine a few more times until Waltman, who had been following, spoke out.

"You wait here," he said. "I'll see if I can get it."

The sorrel played the same game with the man on the horse, pulling away each time he rode up and reached over to grab the reins. At length the big man took down his rope, shook out a loop, and roped the sorrel. With an air of self-satisfaction, he led the horse back to where Spencer stood.

"Don't get on until I've got my rope coiled up," he said.

Spencer grabbed the trailing reins, loosened the rope from around the horse's neck, and tossed the loop and slack over to Waltman. More than once he thought of the pistol wrapped up in the valise, but with the way the slicker and its bundle were tied on top of the satchel, he knew he had no chance of getting the gun out in time to do him any good.

Waltman finished coiling his rope and tied it in place on the saddle. "Get on," he said, "and don't turn him around. We're gonna go west."

This last statement struck Spencer as odd, but he said nothing as he set his reins in place and grabbed the saddle horn. Taking a deep breath and bracing himself against the pain, he poked his boot into the stirrup and swung his leg up and over the bundle. To his surprise, the horse kept still.

The two riders headed west, with the sorrel stepping out ahead while Waltman and the chestnut lagged half a length behind.

Spencer had no idea of where they were headed. If Waltman wanted to take him in for investigation, they should be going either northeast

to town or southeast to the ranch. West made
no sense.

After a couple of miles, Waltman spoke.
"Head toward the south and go between those
two hills," he said.

Now Spencer began to get an inkling. Past
those two hills lay the gully where the A-J men
took horses to cull them. It was an out-of-the-
way place where hardly anyone bothered to go.

Coming out on the other side of the hills,
Spencer saw the gully stretching out below him
on the right. Bleached bones, some brighter than
others in the sunlight, lay scattered where the
coyotes had dragged them.

"Ride down in there," said Waltman.

Spencer turned off the trail and nudged the
sorrel down into the dry wash.

"Hold it there, and get down."

Spencer dismounted and stood with the reins
in his hands as Waltman came to a stop and
pointed his pistol.

"I meant to tell you," he said, in his superior
tone. "I don't think that coat looks very good on
you. I want you to take it off and change it for
that other one you got."

Spencer took off the denim coat and hung it
on the saddle horn with Perk's hat on top. Still
holding the reins, he untied his bundled slicker
and unwrapped the sheepskin coat. As he put
on the coat, Waltman spoke again.

"And while you're at it, untie that grip and set
it on the ground."

Spencer turned and gave him a cross look.
"What for?"

"Don't worry. You won't need it."

This is it, thought Spencer. Waltman was going to sluice him right here and put the valise back under his cot in the bunkhouse. Spencer draped the slicker over the saddle, and with his back to Waltman he untied the leather strings that held the bag in place.

His left hand, which held the reins, rested on the seat of the saddle and touched the slicker. His right hand settled on the handle of the valise. Might as well, he thought. He had nothing to lose.

Dropping the reins and clutching the slicker, he pulled on the valise and bounced it across the sorrel's hip. As the horse jumped forward, Spencer hollered, "Damn!" At the same time, he shook the slicker with his left hand and flung the satchel up and around at Waltman. The sorrel spooked as he had hoped, while Waltman, trying to watch everything at once, leaned back and swiped with the barrel of his pistol as the leather bag sailed at him.

Spencer tossed the slicker in the air for more distraction and jumped in front of Waltman's horse, which had reared back but not up. Spencer grabbed the reins and pulled them from Waltman's hand.

Everything was in motion now, almost chaos except that Spencer held the reins. The horse was stutter-stepping while Spencer pulled on the reins and moved in a circle to his right. Waltman, swaying, was leaned forward in the saddle, aiming his pistol at where Spencer had gone under the horse's jaw and neck. Spencer kept pulling on the reins, trying to keep Waltman off balance and himself shielded by the horse's head and neck as he reached to lay his hand on the stock of the rifle.

As he yanked the rifle free, he pulled straight down on the reins and stopped the horse short. Waltman teetered, still searching with his pistol on the off side of the horse. Spencer stepped back, levered a shell into the Winchester, and was just bringing it above waist level when Waltman came up and brought the pistol around and over the horse's arched neck. Spencer did not have time to raise the rifle and draw a bead. Aiming with his hands and clamping the stock with his right elbow, he pulled the trigger.

Everything came apart now. The rifle roared, the blast threw Waltman backward, and his pistol fired upward as the chestnut reared up, then cut to the right and plunged away. Spencer jacked in another shell and held the rifle ready as the horse galloped off and the scene cleared. Waltman had hit the ground right after the horse jumped, and now he lay still. His hat had rolled a couple of yards away and settled with the crown sticking straight up.

Spencer waited a long moment until he was sure Waltman wasn't going to move. A relaxed stillness settled on the body, and the wool coat lay wide open. Blood had seeped out onto the man's shirtfront, and the string tag on his sack of tobacco dangled from his vest pocket.

Spencer's mouth had gone dry, and his hands were trembling. It had all happened just like that, with no time to think. He had acted on impulse and reflex, that was all, and none too soon.

He did not like having to shoot and kill a man, but he had no room for regret. Waltman had brought him here to leave him for the buzzards and coyotes, so the big man was getting what he had planned to dish out.

Spencer took a deep breath and tried to collect his thoughts. He needed to get his horse—no, he needed to get his gun first, then the horse. He didn't know about the rifle. It would come in handy, but it was heavy, and he didn't have a scabbard on his saddle. Waltman's was long gone.

He made himself start over again. He needed to find his pistol. There was Waltman's lying in the dirt. He could use it if he had to, but he didn't care for the idea. He already had one dead man's gun, and he didn't need another. Besides, he couldn't trust the one on the ground until he had time to clean it. He didn't need a gun that might jam on him. Where was his?

He went and stood over Waltman's body, wondering if the man had stuffed the gun out of sight. Spencer prodded with the toe of his boot. It wasn't in either pocket of the wool coat, which lay to each side, and it wasn't tucked into the man's waistband. Spencer wondered if Waltman had stowed it in the saddlebag. He couldn't remember. Then he saw it. Right there in Waltman's holster, looking normal. Spencer remembered now.

With the six-gun back in his own holster, he laid the rifle in the crook of Waltman's arm and set out for his horse.

The sorrel was a couple of hundred yards away, head down and grazing. Spencer decided to get the horse first and then pick up Perk's coat and hat, which had fallen off at separate points in the commotion.

This time the sorrel let him walk right up and grab the reins. Picking up the hat and coat on the way, Spencer led the horse back to the spot where his belongings lay.

Again he made himself think things out, get them into a deliberate sequence. First he checked the rigging to see if anything was out of order. It looked all right, so he cinched up. Then he loaded his gear on again, starting with the leather gripsack and laying the sheepskin coat wrapped in the slicker on top of that. He tied the saddle strings tight.

As he put on the denim coat, he decided to wear Perk's dark brown hat instead of his own of plain brown. Perk's had a larger crown and brim, and together with the coat it would be less likely to give him away at a distance. Stowing his own hat, he pulled on the other one. It fit all right.

He walked the sorrel horse away from the scene, but before trying to mount up he took a final glance around. Waltman's pistol lay in the dirt where it had fallen, and the rifle rested in the crook of his arm. The dead man lay faceup to the sun. The rough texture of his features, combined with his thick head of short, coarse hair, made him look like a tomcat laid out for his last long sleep.

For a moment, Spencer felt a small pang of remorse. It was too bad things had gone this way, but it was either Waltman or himself. The big man had set things up that way, with no other choice, and there was no changing the outcome.

Spencer told himself he couldn't dwell on it any longer. For one thing, he was sure Waltman was not acting on his own initiative. For another, he imagined Waltman's horse was headed back to the A-J with an empty saddle. Spencer knew that if he was going to stay a jump ahead of Al Jerome, he was going to have to keep on the move.

Even though the sorrel had given him no trouble when he caught the horse and loaded on his gear again, the animal still wanted to step away on him when he tried to mount up. After a few tries he walked the horse in a circle once, twice, and came to a stop. He put his foot in the stirrup, hung on to reins and mane and saddle horn, and swung up and over.

The horse took off at a fast walk right away, and Spencer let him keep that pace as long as he did not bolt. The sorrel went up the wash and out through the pass between the hills. Spencer did not look back at the boneyard. He had to keep his mind on the horse and on what lay ahead. It occurred to him that he had done something, a large thing in itself, but in comparison with what was still out there, it wasn't much.

Chapter Thirteen

Spencer rode northeast with the midday sun over his shoulder. The sky had cleared out, and the sunshine was warmer now. The wind was not so sharp, as only a slight breeze moved across the grass in front of him. The day seemed to be shaping up as one in which a light warmth would stay around from late morning to midafternoon. Spencer thought of it as a convenient time for riders to be out, and it was conducive to a lone wolf gunman who might linger on the sunny side of a little bluff—if he knew where Spencer was riding. Spencer hoped the man had gone up to the Bates place and waited for the sunrise there, but he knew that men like Carlton kept at their best game by showing up unexpected.

As Spencer reined the horse to one side and then another to go through a patch of sagebrush, he caught a glimpse of his own shadow. The tall crown and wide brim looked unusual, and the image reminded Spencer that he owed an incalculable debt to the happy kid whose life had been cut all too short.

Now more than ever, Spencer was convinced that Wolf Carlton had fired the fatal shot and had intended it for him. He was also convinced that Al Jerome had hired the killer to do it, just as he had no doubt put Waltman up to looking for Spencer and making the move he had attempted. Waltman had been so sure of himself that he hadn't tried very hard to conceal his intentions, which included getting hold of the leather valise. That detail in itself told Spencer that Waltman knew how things had gone with Cliff Ardmore and that Waltman had been in on planting the revolver in Spencer's bag. So much for that. The bunkhouse bully was through with his maneuvers. Still, there remained the question of how much Kern and Galloway knew about the state of affairs. Spencer figured he would be able to know that as soon as he saw them again.

Meanwhile, his main interest was in keeping to open country as much as he could and then ride into town in broad daylight. There, as he had told Eva earlier in the day, he could try to find out why Al Jerome would turn on one of his own kind and have Cliff Ardmore put away for good.

Spencer made it to town without incident, having paused a mile out to put on his own hat and coat. Once in town, he left his horse in the livery stable and set out on foot. Not much was going on in the main street. Here and there a horse stood tied at a hitching rail, and a wagon was drawn up in front of the mercantile. As usual, men loitered here and there in doorways and on benches in front of businesses, but no one paid him much attention.

He walked the two and a half blocks to the Paragon Hotel, where a desk clerk with a graying beard and a spreading girth was examining a photograph with a magnifying glass. He set the items aside, raised his head, and adjusted his necktie.

"Yes, sir?" he called out, giving Spencer a look of appraisal.

Not wishing to speak any louder than he had to, Spencer walked right up to the counter and said, "I was wondering if I might find Mrs. Ardmore here. I was told she had taken a room in this place."

The man gave him another looking-over, as if for the first time, and then in a matter-of-fact tone he answered, "She stays here."

Sensing that the clerk liked to be difficult, Spencer made an effort to be precise as he phrased his question. "Would it be possible to let her know that I was hoping to be able to speak with her?"

The man pursed his lips and put on an innocent expression. "Refer to you by name, or just tell her there's a man here?"

"Oh, give her my name. It's Spencer Prescott."

The clerk stretched his chin forward and up about half an inch, then brought it back to its usual position. "I can do that. Don't know how long it will be, though. I believe she's got a visitor at the moment."

"Oh." Spencer wondered if Al Jerome had come to town today.

The man raised his head in an attitude of casual authority. "You can have a seat if you wish." He tipped his head to the left, where a sitting area was illuminated only by light coming in through the front window.

Spencer recognized the area from the day he came here to tell Eva Wingate about her husband. From all that had happened in the meanwhile, that meeting seemed to be far in the past.

Spencer took the first seat he came to, a dark wooden chair with armrests. As soon as he settled in, he saw that he could have sat in one of the more comfortable upholstered chairs. It didn't matter. He stayed where he was and took off his hat.

A quarter of an hour went by. The clerk had taken out a ledger and put on a pair of spectacles. With his tongue between his lips and with an occasional stretching of his neck, he perused the pages, turning them one way and the other as he went forward and backward in his study.

Movement caught Spencer's eye. A man came into view on the stairway, a man in a gray wool suit. He had just finished settling a short-brimmed hat on his head, and his bronzed complexion was visible as he raised his chin. Coming down the staircase, he had a spring in his step as he put one polished foot and then another on the carpeted stairs. He had a husky, athletic posture with his shoulders squared and his arms hanging loose, as if he was ready to take up a racquet or a bat. At the bottom of the stairway he tossed a glance of recognition at the clerk, then turned and went out the front door. The man had such a light air about him that Spencer wondered if he had come on legal business.

About a minute after the lawyer had gone out the door, the clerk stretched out his chin, brought it back, and closed the ledger. He stowed the volume beneath the counter, then left his post and went up the stairs in short, measured steps.

A few minutes later he came back down and said, "Mrs. Ardmore can see you now." He paused long enough for Spencer to rise and come forward. Then he turned and mounted the stairs as before, leaving Spencer to catch up as he might.

At the landing, the clerk turned right and followed a strip of dark green carpet down a shadowy hallway. About halfway to the end, the man paused at a door on his left and rapped on the panel.

A woman's voice from inside called, "Come in."

The clerk opened the door and stood to one side as he motioned for Spencer to pass through.

The room was lit up by an oil lamp as well as by sunlight coming in through a window at the back of the room. At a glance, Spencer saw that he was in the first of more than one room, with a door on the right that no doubt led to a bedroom. This room was furnished with a stuffed chair on either side of the closed bedroom door, two wooden chairs with padded seats against the far wall, a low table in the middle of the room, and a fold-down desk against the left wall. Seated sideways by the desk, in the posture of a person who had turned from looking over some papers, was Julia Ardmore. She rose and faced him as the door behind him closed.

She looked as if she had taken the recent course of events in good stride. Her blonde hair, clean and full-bodied, hung loose to her shoulders. Her dark blue eyes had a shine to them, and her face had a healthy glow. She was wearing a light blue dress that looked fresh and clean, as if she had just put it on and was on her way to a tea. It was a high-necked dress with a close bodice, and it showed her figure to advantage.

"How do you do, Mr. Prescott?" she said in a pleasant voice. "Please have a seat." With her left hand open she gestured toward the two padded chairs.

He remembered their earlier meeting, how he had called her "ma'am" and she had said he could call her Julia, but he could tell right away that they had gone back to a less familiar footing. He said, "Thank you, ma'am, and thank you for agreeing to see me. I didn't know if you cared to have anything to do with men off the range."

She gave a clever smile. "Nothing wrong with you, I hope."

"No, ma'am," he said, laughing. "Nothing that would be a danger to you."

She sat down, and when he had done likewise, she raised her eyebrows and said, "And how can I be of help to you today?"

He hesitated. "Well, Mrs. Ardmore," he began, "I hope you don't find me objectionable. If anything I say or ask makes you uncomfortable, please let me know. I didn't come here to trouble you."

She waved her hand in a small gesture of dismissal. "If you've come to ask me something, I imagine you've got trouble enough for yourself. So I'll guess we're on even terms."

"Thanks for seeing it that way." He put his hat on his knee, then took it away and held it next to the leg of his chair. Sensing that she was waiting for him to state his business, he said, "Well, I guess I should get to the point, but I don't want to be blunt. But enough things have gone on, or I should say, things have gone so far, that—"

"Please go ahead and be blunt," she said, with a smile of encouragement.

He heaved a breath. "As you know all too well, men have lost their lives in the last few months, and the ones who should be doing something about it aren't doing much. The sheriff treats it as if it's two sides trying to even the score up against one another, but that doesn't match with what I've seen."

She gave him her attention. "And what have you seen?"

He hadn't planned the order in which he was going to present things, much less the words he was going to use, and now he felt stupid for not having come prepared. He looked straight at the woman and said, "A young fella who rode with me, a harmless kid named Millard Perkins, was shot in the back right outside a line shack while I was inside."

The woman had a pained expression on her face as she shook her head. "I'm sorry to hear that. It's one more senseless death."

"That it is, and furthermore, I'm convinced the bullet was meant for me."

She stared at him as she took in an audible breath with her lips parted, and then she found words. "How sure are you?"

"Pretty sure, I'd say."

"Do you have any idea who might have done it?" she asked. The tone of her voice and the look in her eyes conveyed a feeling of trust.

He nodded. "I do. Not just who did it but who was behind it. But as you can imagine, it's not something I should blurt out. For one thing, I don't have proof, and for another, I don't know how you would take it."

She arched her brows. "If by that you mean I would be offended on behalf of some affiliation, let me tell you, I've had very little benefit of that in the past couple of months."

"That doesn't surprise me." He thought for a couple of seconds. "Let me put it this way. I think the sheriff's theory of two sides going at each other is flawed. I've got a suspicion that the same person who was behind the deaths of George Farrow and Collins Wingate was also behind your husband's."

She showed little emotion as she said, "To borrow your phrase, that doesn't surprise me."

"If that's so, then I've got all the more reason to believe that the same person wanted to get me out of the way."

She tipped her head. "Why?"

Spencer leveled his gaze. "Among other things, he might not have wanted me collecting impressions from you or anyone else. More than that, I think he wanted to make it look as if I had done in your husband, and if he could shut me up for good, he might have a better chance of getting it to stick." From her expression he gathered that she was open to his interpretation, so he went on. "I came here thinking that if this made sense to you, I might learn something that would help me—help me confirm that I'm on the right track and maybe help me decide what to do next."

"If it makes sense to me, which I can say it does, then I would guess we've got the same person in mind." She shifted in her seat and tossed him a light smile. "But neither of us wants to be the first to say it out loud."

He nodded with a faint smile in return.

"It reminds me of my Aunt Jenny."

"In what way?" he asked.

"Well, my Aunt Jenny—how shall I put it— had a friend named Alice James. Doesn't that seem at all germane?"

Spencer's eyes met hers in confidence. "Oh, I should say so." Again he was careful to pick through his words. "What I'd like to know, then, or get a better idea of, is what the man's motives would have been. To all appearances, he acted as if someone got at a close ally of his and made him worry for his own life."

"Sure," said Mrs. Ardmore. "He kept up a front."

"But they were close friends, weren't they? That was the way it seemed when your husband came to the A-J and when we were all on round-up after that."

"You're right. They were friends. Close associates."

"Excuse me if I put it too strongly, but some people would say they were in cahoots."

She gave a light toss of the head. "It's in the past, and I don't see much point in trying to pretend they weren't. I won't ask who those 'some people' were, but I could guess."

It was his turn to shrug. "That's in the past, too, in something of the same sense. I heard it from one of George Farrow's men and from Collins Wingate. They both believed—and again, I don't want to go too far—that these two associates were also in cahoots with a stock detective who has a talent for—"

"For taking care of problems," she said.

"That's very much like the way I heard it. The rustler problem."

"I'm sorry to say it—no, really, I'm ashamed to say it—but they were probably not wrong." After what seemed like a moment's hesitation, she went further. "They had him keeping an eye on the so-called rustlers and whoever associated with them. Of course, Cliff got around and kept his lookout as well."

"So they would have had me pegged early on."

She tipped her head side to side, and her blonde hair waved. "I would suppose so, if you fraternized very much with those others."

Her words gave Spencer pause. "That's the same word the boss used," he said. "Did you hear it used by someone?"

"I think that's the way I heard it put."

Spencer's eyes went to the ceiling and came back down. "Again, that doesn't surprise me very much. And after all, I was friends with Collins Wingate, not just a casual acquaintance like I was with Farrow's men."

She gave a small nod, encouraging him to go on.

"Wingate's idea, and mine, too, as time went on, was that these cattlemen had their little syndicate and had taken courage from what others had gotten away with. In the case over on the Sweetwater, for example, they ended up with the property of the woman they hanged, in addition to getting away with the lynching itself. It seemed like that incident, and the business in Johnson County, gave these fellows the idea that they could do as they wanted."

Mrs. Ardmore's tongue showed as she took a breath. "I don't know how much they were influenced," she said, "but they did seem to think that way, that they could do as they pleased."

Spencer gave her a close look. "It wasn't just power or control, then, was it? It was property, too."

She looked down and nodded. "That's right. Cliff was supposed to get the Farrow place, and his associate was supposed to end up with Wingate's. But there were two problems. For one, Mrs. Wingate didn't give up and leave soon enough, and for another, Cliff thought his associate was getting a better deal, even though it hadn't come into his hands yet."

"And that's why Cliff went wheedling?"

Mrs. Ardmore gave a sad smile. "You knew Cliff. He usually had more than one motive going on with something like that. But, yes, he didn't think he was getting his fair share out of the plan, so he tried to get an advantage on his own."

"And then his partner didn't like Cliff turning on him, so he repaid him in kind."

She blinked and said, "That's the way it seems. Ironic, you might say. Cliff felt he was being cheated. He used to say it was good to be cheated once in a while because it kept you sharp, but he resented his partner doing it to him. And he didn't see himself as doing anything like that, of course."

"I'm sure." After a brief reflection, Spencer said, "I'm surprised he told you as much as he did."

She waved her hand. "Oh, I'm sure there was plenty he didn't tell me. And he had a reason for telling me what he did. He was very emphatic that I was not supposed to know any of this, and he was only telling me in case something should happen to him."

"And something did."

"That's right."

"But it hasn't done any good, your knowing."

"No, not yet. I think like you do in this respect, if I understand you right. Sheriff Ross doesn't seem to want to know everything, and I think it's because he's thick with the owner of the A-J. If I tell him everything I think I know, not only does it stand a good chance of going to waste, but it could come back to get me as well."

Spencer frowned. "But don't you have a lawyer who could look out for you in that way? Protect your rights?"

For just a second she gave him a curious look. Then she said, "I do have a lawyer who looks after my interests, but they have more to do with assets and property. I don't know if he handles criminal matters, and to tell you the truth, I don't know how much I want to be entailed in something like that."

"Oh."

She said nothing, as if she was waiting for him to say more.

"And yet you've been forward enough with me," he said.

She looked straight at him. "Unless I miss my guess by a long ways, you're not in a position where selling me out would do you any good." Her face relaxed into a smile. "And besides, I think you've got too much honor for that."

He returned the smile. "Thanks. And there is a chance that what you know will help set things right."

She seemed to lose a bit of her jauntiness for a moment. Her eyes were moist as she said, "You know, Mr. Prescott, even if Cliff was a cad to me and a conspirator against these smaller ranchers, he didn't deserve to die by this kind of treachery. Whoever did it should be brought to account."

"I'm in complete agreement with that." He tried to sort through his words again. "But supposing I was in a position to do something, and you could be sure none of this could come back on you. Would you be willing to tell what you know?"

The question seemed to give her discomfort. "I don't know. I couldn't say for sure. It would depend on how things looked when the time came. You now how these men can be. If there was any chance he could wiggle free—well, you mentioned that case where they took over the woman's property. As I recall, one or two witnesses disappeared as well. So I would have to be cautious about coming forward with damning evidence."

"Well, it's just a thought. He'd have to be locked up good and tight, and we're still a long ways away from that."

She gave him a matter-of-fact look. "That's true. I told you what I did because I hoped it might help get him there. If it helps you deal with some of your own difficulties, so much the better. I gather that's why you came, not as a crusader for higher justice."

He shrugged. "Well, partly. But—"

"Don't apologize. We've all got to look out for ourselves. I've already told you I've done it myself, and if I have to do it again, I will. But I trust you won't misuse what I've imparted."

"I'll try not to. I'm not one to spill the beans."

She smiled. "I didn't think so."

"And while we're at it," he said, "is there anything you'd like to ask me? Seems only fair."

"No," she answered, shaking her head. "I'm not very inquisitive, and I've usually been better off not knowing about men's affairs."

He raised his eyebrows. "Well, then, I won't take up any more of your time. I appreciate your help. It's considerate of you."

She had her clever smile again, hardened a little. "Just a piece of goodwill on my part, with the hopes that it will help hang a man who deserves it."

He rose and gave her his hand as she remained seated. "Thanks again," he said. "I hope something good comes of it."

"Good luck," she answered.

He went out the door, into the shadowy hallway. He put on his hat just before he reached the stairway, then watched the lobby come into view as he went down the stairs. No one was in attendance at the reception desk, so he turned and walked out of the building.

The sun hadn't moved much in the short time he had been visiting with Mrs. Ardmore. On his way into town, for lack of a more definite plan, he had assumed he would go on up to the line camp, but now he felt himself resisting the idea. He didn't like the prospect of traveling in that vicinity at nightfall, and now, with the improved understanding he had just gotten, he thought it might be best to pay another visit to the A-J before much more time elapsed.

As he walked along the sidewalk on the north side of the street, he cast his glance over the horses tied at the hitching rails. Up ahead, in front of the Horseshoe Saloon, he saw two horses he thought he recognized.

Closer, he confirmed his impression. The first horse was a dull, muddy-colored bay that Galloway rode. The other was a thin-haired sorrel from Kern's string, and as further evidence it had his rough-leather Mother Hubbard saddle on its back. Spencer figured this was as good a place as any to find out how the cards lay, so he turned into the doorway of the Horseshoe and pushed the door.

Inside, as his eyes adjusted, he saw Kern and Galloway standing at the bar. Galloway seemed to flinch at seeing who came in, but he raised his hand in greeting. Spencer returned the gesture and walked toward them.

The two punchers had all the appearance of being caught at something. Galloway looked at his drink and then turned to face Spencer. He stood straight up, striking the pose of a man in uniform with his black stovepipe boots, the black vest of matching tone, his cross-draw pistol, and his black hat with the straight narrow brim. Kern, who stood slouching in drab clothes and his funnel-brimmed hat, looked as if he might have been the hostler for the horse guards.

"Well, hallo, Spencer," said Galloway. "Surprised to see you here."

"Likewise. I saw your horses, so I thought I should stop in."

Galloway turned down the corners of his mouth and gave a slight toss of the head. "We came in right ahead of you. Just stopped in for a quick one." His eyes flickered away and came back. "Al sent us into town on an errand."

"Oh."

Galloway nodded. "Uh-huh. He sent us in with Perk's effects, includin' a letter from home that has his ma's address. He was from Canton, Ohio, you know."

"I remember that."

"So Al sent his address, and what few things he had, along with enough money to ship the body home."

Spencer nodded. The mention of those details brought back the numb, hollow feeling from before.

Galloway went on. "Al feels just turrible about it. Ever'one liked that kid."

"I know." Spencer felt a lump in his throat as he spoke.

"How 'bout yourself?"

"Me?"

"I mean, how'd you come to be in town? We thought you'd be up at the Bates place."

"I was. But I found something I thought the sheriff should know about. It was a Winchester rifle casing. I brought it in to show him, and I was on my way back out when I saw you fellas' horses." Spencer motioned for three drinks. Then he gave Kern a glance of recognition and spoke again to Galloway. "What's new at the ranch? I would've thought Al and Dick would have come in and left you two to do the work."

Galloway appraised the second drink being set in front of him, then wrinkled his nose as he answered, "Al sent Dick down to Alderman's, and I think he wanted to wait around to see what Dick had to say when he got back."

"Probably so." Spencer laid a silver dollar on the bar and picked up his drink. "Here's to Perk," he said.

The three men raised their glasses.

"You bet," said Galloway. "He was a hell of a good kid. I hope whoever did it gets what's comin' to him."

"Ah'd wind the rope muh-seff," said Kern.

Galloway smacked from taking a drink. "Sons a' bitches in this world," he said.

"Too many." Spencer tossed off his drink. "Well, boys, I'd better git. Long ride ahead. We'll see you again real soon."

"Thanks for the drink," said Galloway. "You keep a lookout, now."

"I will."

Kern cleared his throat. "Thanks for the drink," he said.

"My pleasure." Spencer held up his hand. "So long, boys." He walked out of the Horseshoe and turned right on the sidewalk. He was glad to have gotten out of the saloon ahead of the others, and he was satisfied with what he learned. Now he needed to hole up in the livery stable until dark. The fall off the horse had given him some sore spots on top of the others, and he didn't know how long of a night he had ahead of him. A little rest would do him good.

Chapter Fourteen

Spencer waited in the shadows until Jerome left the bunkhouse, went into the ranch house, and lit a lamp. A quarter moon hung almost straight up in the sky, so Spencer could see objects and movement. He had left the sorrel in the barn, saddled, in case he needed to make a fast get-away, but he planned to change to a fresh horse if he was not in a hurry. It depended on how things went with Jerome.

As he had waited, Spencer had speculated on what the scene inside the bunkhouse was like. Jerome, Kern, and Galloway would have been the only men at the table, with Mac the cook standing by. From Spencer's visit in the Horse-shoe Saloon, he was satisfied that Jerome hadn't taken the two hired men into confidence, so the conversation about where Waltman was being detained must have been an interesting one. Now the boss had returned to his own quarters, and Spencer did not know whether Waltman's horse had come back—and if so, how many people knew. From the calmness at the ranch and the routineness of the meal, however, he assumed no one had found the body itself.

Spencer crossed the corner of the yard, went up the two steps, and knocked on the door with his knuckles as he had seen Waltman do.

A quick voice came from within. "Yeah! Come on in!"

As Spencer pushed the door open and stepped inside, the surprise on Al Jerome's face told him the boss was expecting someone else.

"Spencer!" he said, tensing with a frown as he stood behind his desk. "What are you doing here? I thought you were up at Bates." The boss's eyes traveled over the sheepskin coat.

Spencer closed the door with as little noise as possible. "I had to come back, sir. I had something to tell you in the strictest confidence."

Jerome gave him a cross look. The boss had not yet taken off his hat, and the lamplight cast his face in shadow. "What's so secret?" he demanded.

"It's about one of your men."

Jerome's eyes narrowed. "Which one?"

"Dick Waltman, sir. You know, he took it into his head to give me a thrashing yesterday evening."

"I don't know anything about that."

Spencer doubted it, but he didn't mind playing along. "The others could tell you. They watched."

"That doesn't concern me very much, and I don't see where it's a reason for you to come on some secret errand when you're supposed to be up north working—unless you just want to talk behind his back."

Spencer shook his head. "That's not it, sir. I told you that much to give you some background on what happened next."

Jerome's eyebrows flickered. "What's that?"

"Well, he must not have been satisfied with knocking me down a few times, for he came after me this morning."

"He did?" The boss's eyes were quick and close.

"Yes, sir. Just as I was leaving town. You see, I put up in town last night. I was too roughed up to make it all the way, so I stayed over and set out north this morning. Right outside of town he caught up with me and braced me."

"The hell. He must have ridden pretty damn fast. He had breakfast here." Jerome looked skeptical.

"He was riding that long-legged chestnut, and it was pretty well lathered." Spencer shrugged. "And I guess I didn't get out of town quite at the crack of dawn."

"Yeah, yeah," said Jerome. "So what happened? You say he pulled a gun on you?"

"Not at first. He just started flingin' accusations. Didn't make any sense at all."

"Accusations. About what?"

"Oh, about me bein' in cahoots with rustlers. You know there's nothin' to that."

Jerome turned his head so that his reddish brown hair shone in the lamplight. "It's hard to know what anyone knows for sure," he said.

"Maybe so. But I still thought it was pretty cheeky of him to turn on one of his fellow riders like that. The way I see it, if I ride for you, and he turns on me, then he's a turncoat to the whole outfit."

"Oh, no," said Jerome. "Someone as trusted as Dick wouldn't do something like that. If he had a suspicion about you, he would have had a reason."

"I don't know, sir. But he was acting mighty strange. Had a glint in his eye."

Jerome's voice was curt as he said, "Well, where is he?"

"He's with Sheriff Ross, sir. I had to take him in, he was actin' so uncivil and sayin' such far-fetched things."

"Such as?"

"Like I said. Me bein' a rustler. Why, the closest I ever came to that was brandin' mavericks for you."

Jerome flinched.

"And Dick, he did it right along with me. You know that. And then for him to say that about me—why, that's not straight."

The tip of Jerome's nose showed in the lantern light as he shifted in his stance. "If Dick has suspicions, they might be warranted. After all, you *have* been pretty chummy with the rustler element, and I've told you that myself."

"I don't know that they are, or were, rustlers, but that's another argument." Spencer put on a casual expression. "Mainly I came to let you know about your hired man."

The boss's eyes traveled over Spencer again, from his hat down to the bottom of his coat. "You're the one who sounds daft," he said. "What did Ross say about this? I can't believe he took Dick in."

Spencer scratched his temple with his left hand. "Well, Dick was a little groggy. You see, he tried to take a shot at me—that's why I thought he might be off his bean—and his horse reared up and dumped him, gave him quite a knock on the head. The horse took off south at a dead run, so I got Dick up onto my horse and took him into town. Took a while. His tongue was still pretty thick when the sheriff got him into a cell. If he comes around and talks sense, which he may have done by now, maybe the sheriff'll listen to him."

Jerome's face went back into shadow. "Why didn't Ross tell Scot about it this afternoon?"

"Oh, I think the sheriff was probably keepin' it under his hat. He's got to know that the only way to get to the bottom of things is to listen to all sides."

"This still doesn't make sense," said Jerome, shaking his head. "None at all."

Spencer raised his eyebrows and tipped his head. "Well, it does to me. Too much, actually."

The cross look came again. "What do you mean?"

After a measured breath, Spencer said, "I think Dick was out to get me, one way or the other. And I think that was because someone else tried to get me and got Perk instead."

"Ah, you're all wet."

"You think so? Then why would someone want to shoot that kid?"

"Bah," Jerome scoffed. "You never know. This kid Perkins was new and unknown. I never saw him do anything out of the way here, but that doesn't mean he didn't have it in him. Like as not, he got run off from some other outfit, just like Trask got run off from here."

Spencer thought it was cheap of Jerome to say that, and it sure didn't match with how "turrible" the boss felt, according to Galloway. "Everyone's got an opinion," said Spencer. "I thought the kid was all right and Dick was up to somethin'."

"Well, you'll get straight on that," said Jerome. He picked up a brass cylindrical object from the blotter on his desk and hefted it in his palm, as if out of curiosity. It looked like a pendulum weight, and Spencer assumed it served the function of a paperweight on the boss's desk.

"I might. But I wonder why he left me this." Spencer reached into the pocket of his coat and brought out the ivory-handled revolver, and with one smooth motion he leveled it at the man across from him.

Jerome's eyes went wide open. "Where did you get that?"

"I believe Dick Waltman left it in my leather valise. If he didn't, he at least knew about it, because he tried to take the satchel from me."

"You know whose that looks like." Jerome pointed his chin at the gun, and his voice had a reprimanding tone to it.

"Oh, sure. And I think someone planted it on me to try to make me look like the one who did in your associate."

Jerome hefted the brass weight. "Maybe you did. The sheriff knows you had motives."

"People have told him that, and that's what Waltman tried to tell me, but it just made me think someone has it all rehearsed."

Jerome shifted his feet again. "Like you said,

everyone's got an opinion. There's more than one theory about who killed Cliff Ardmore and why he would want to, but they tend to lead back to you more than anyone else."

"As far as that goes, they lead back to you pretty well."

Jerome scowled. "Oh, go on. There's nothing to that. We were the best of friends."

"Up to a point, I guess."

Jerome looked at the pistol and said, "What point?"

Spencer had not eared back the hammer, and he didn't want to if he didn't have to. A gunshot was more than likely to bring the other two hired hands on a run. "I think you know what I mean," he said.

"I'll be damned if I do."

Spencer pursed his lips. "Have you thought of engaging a lawyer?"

Jerome's hand went still, and he gave Spencer a curious look. "What the hell for?"

"Well, what I'm plannin' to do is take you into town so you can talk to the sheriff, too."

"I think you're out of your depth here, Spencer. You've got no authority. You're not a lawman."

"That's what I told Dick, and he laughed at me, until I turned things around."

"Well, you can turn around yourself. I've got nothin' more to say to the sheriff."

"You might, when he asks you some questions."

"About what?" Jerome hefted the brass weight again and shifted his position so that he stood at the corner of the desk.

"About the scheme you had with your best of friends. How you were going to divvy up these other men's property, and then how you didn't like it when he tried to get the best of the deal."

Jerome's face stiffened, and the brass object settled in his hand. "I don't let men talk to me that way," he said. "Especially hired men."

"Tell that to Waltman."

"What do you mean?"

"You might be sharin' a cell with him. Like I told you, I'm takin' you in."

"You'll be sorry you tried."

All this time, Spencer had noticed that Jerome was wearing his gun belt but had his coat buttoned so that only the tip of his holster showed. "Let's not both be sorry," Spencer replied. "I'd be sorry if you ended up with a hole in you like Waltman did."

Jerome arched his brows but held stiff.

Spencer continued. "Don't unbutton your coat. With your left hand, unbuckle your gun belt and lower it to the floor. Then put your toy back on the desktop."

Jerome did as he was told, up to pulling off the gun belt, but instead of setting it on the floor he held it out at arm's length and moved toward a chair that sat a couple of paces away from the side of his desk. As he angled forward, he dropped the belt so that the holster clunked on the edge of the chair. With that distraction he came around with his right fist, which was closed upon the brass weight.

The impact felt like a lump of iron hitting Spencer's jaw and shaking his head back. The revolver clattered to the floor as he took half a step back, and then Jerome was upon him.

Both men had lost their hats, and it was a close-in struggle now. Jerome seemed intent on settling things with his two hands. He yanked Spencer by the coat collar and hammered his cheek and jawbone twice more with the ironlike fist. Spencer hooked his left arm up, under, over, and around Jerome's right arm, then clamped down. Wedging his right arm between his chest and Jerome's, he pulled down hard and broke the other man's grip. The brass weight thudded on the floor, and Spencer kicked it aside as he pushed free.

Jerome came up and rushed him again, this time tackling him to the floor. He tried to get both hands on Spencer's throat, but Spencer bucked with his hips and shoved the man off to the side. He brought up a boot and pushed against Jerome, then rolled to the other side and came up in a crouch.

Jerome had come up as well, and in his hand he held a fireplace poker with an iron hook on the heavy tip.

The first swipe cut the air next to Spencer's temple, so he ducked aside and tried to straighten up inside his coat, which had twisted on him in the scuffle. His gun, as Jerome's had been, was covered by the skirt of his coat, and he would have to fumble to get at it. In addition, he still did not want to fire a shot unless he had no other way.

Jerome had his face bunched in fury as he closed in with another swing. Spencer threw up his left arm and felt the whack of the iron against the bone of his forearm. Ducking and dodging, he moved to the side of the room that had been at his back when he came in. A new saddle sat atop a three-tier stack of bulging burlap grain sacks, and standing in the shadowy corner of the room was a heavy livestock cane. About five feet tall and an inch thick all the way along, it looked like a brute version of the shepherd staffs in Bible illustrations. It had a simple crook with no recurve, and to Spencer it was as welcome as a crowbar.

He grabbed it and took a hold with both hands. As Jerome came in for his third strike with the poker, Spencer stepped back and aside. With a swing, he caught the hooked iron tip against the wooden crook of the cane, and with a quick yank he pulled the poker from Jerome's hands and sent it bouncing on the floor. As he drew the cane back for another swing, Jerome produced a small pistol, the size of a .32, from inside his coat. Spencer swung with all his force.

The thick head of the cane hit Jerome at the base of the skull behind his left ear, and it felled him like a poleaxed steer.

Spencer stood back and pulled in gulps of air. The room had gone silent except for his own breathing. No sounds came from the ranch yard. He expected to hear voices, or the slamming of a door, or the commotion of horses, but he heard nothing to suggest that the brawl had gone beyond these four walls.

From where he stood, he observed the body laid out on the floor. It did not move. He could not detect the slightest rise and fall of breathing. Rather, the body was limp and sprawled, just as it had fallen.

Spencer cast around until he saw the ivory-handled pistol on the floor. He went to it and picked it up, spun the cylinder, and put it in his coat pocket once again.

A plan was beginning to form, now that the confrontation with Jerome had taken its course. The boss wasn't going to be able to answer any questions now, but he could do one little job, serve one purpose, for the greater good.

In the next few minutes, Spencer put things in order. He set the poker by the fireplace and stood the livestock cane in its corner. He found the brass weight where it had rolled away during the struggle, and he put it back on the desk. He straightened the chair and picked up Jerome's gun belt. It could go with the body, along with the hat, so if someone came looking for the boss, it would seem as if he left on business. As Spencer pulled the body around to prop it up, the little .32 hideout gun rolled free. He stuck it back in Jerome's shoulder holster.

Spencer blew out the lamp and waited. Time dragged on, slow and haunting, after the violent struggle. From his seat by the front window he could see the bunkhouse, and when the last glow of light went out, he set to work.

First he went to the corral and brought the dark horse into the barn. He transferred all of his gear from the sorrel, which had seen plenty of work in the last twenty-four hours. He turned the sorrel into the corral and caught a dark horse

from Jerome's string. Back in the barn he saddled that horse, working more by touch than by
sight. He thought of saddling the horses outside
in the moonlight, but he knew how cowpunch-
ers slept. Any irregular sound might carry, and
to one of the hired hands peering out from the
bunkhouse, he would look like a thief in the
night. Better, he thought, to work slower and in
the dark.

The hardest part was getting Jerome loaded
onto the horse, but Spencer told himself he had
no choice. It had to go this way. With heaving
and struggling and no small amount of persis-
tence, he got the body pushed up and over the
saddle, then tied down.

From the position of the stars and from his
own sense of how much time had elapsed, he
figured it was not quite midnight when he led
the two horses out of the ranch yard. He took
soft steps until he was a hundred yards out.
There he checked the cinches on both horses,
and after turning his own so that he would not
catch his foot in the lead rope, he put his foot
in the stirrup and mounted up. It was going to
be a long, lone ride in the night, and he didn't
have time to spare. He needed to get to the line
camp well before sunup. If he didn't, he could
find himself in a hell of a fix.

In the light of the waning moon, after grain-
ing the two horses waiting in the corral and the
two he came in with, Spencer set things up. He
propped Jerome's body against the corral in a
sitting position where it would be in clear view.

After pulling off the man's dark broadcloth coat and leaving it in the shed with his hat, he put his own hat and sheepskin coat on the dead man. He tipped the hat forward to obscure the features and to make it seem as if the man was asleep. Figuring that was the best he could do, he withdrew into the shed, where he put on Perk's hat and coat, took off his spurs, and wrapped a blanket around himself.

He felt worn out, exhausted, but his nerves were so on edge that he couldn't sleep even if he wanted to. The time of night was strange. It was that time well after midnight but before any hints of dawn—the time when, as people claimed, energy was lowest. Old dogs, old horses, old people—all died at various hours of the day or night, but he had heard it said that they died more often in the early hours. People had other quaint ways of saying it—that it was the time of night when goats or donkeys had their blood in their knees, that it was the time when people's souls slipped away the easiest and the spirits that came for them knew it. To someone just getting up or just going to bed, such as riders coming in from or going out to night herd, it was a known time. The same went for a man who woke in the night at some unfamiliar noise, lay on his back, and after a while went back to sleep. But for people who kept an uncertain vigil—waiting to see if a loved one would come home, hanging on to the hope that a person would live through the night, or trying to comprehend the departure of someone who would breathe no more—for these people, the early hours were not just the darkest before dawn. They were the hours of despair, of drifting, of weariness and loss and feeling lost, where time stretched and thinned out and did not proceed one minute after another.

Spencer's chin dropped, and he jerked awake. He had been wrong again. He thought he couldn't sleep, and here he had gone out like a kitten held down in a horse trough. He had to stay awake. This wasn't just night guard, where his horse might jump out from under him or the cattle might spook. This was the place where someone had wanted to put a bullet between his shoulder blades and would be happy for the chance to try again. He took a deep breath and sat wide-eyed in the dark, waiting.

Chapter Fifteen

In the gray light before dawn he heard the faint tread of footsteps. A horse whickered; hooves shuffled; the body of a large animal in the corral brushed against the corner of the shed. From the opposite direction, another footstep sounded.

Spencer's heart was beating fast, pounding, rising in his chest, and drumming in his ears. His mouth was dry. He moistened his lips and breathed with his mouth open.

As the steps came closer, he lowered the blanket to the floor and shifted so he could see through a crack. Sure enough, it was the man he expected, lean and lethal as he came forward. In the wan morning his dark outfit was visible— the hat with its lengthwise crease, the wool coat open and the gun handle showing, the wool trousers, the narrow boots. He wore gloves and carried a rifle in his right hand, and he kept his eyes fixed ahead of him as he walked forward. Crouched where he was, Spencer had the illusion that Wolf Carlton had come to look at him and shoot him in his grave.

The man stopped in front of the body, and with the tip of the rifle barrel he lifted the hat.

The barrel slipped away, and the hat fell back into place. Steadier, the man lifted the brim again. From a distance of four feet, Spencer heard a short, whiffling sound that a man makes when he sets his upper teeth on his lower lip and blows once, short and low.

"F-f-f."

Carlton straightened up, looked around, and turned. Spencer's heart jumped into a race again as he heard the footsteps come around the corner of the shed. But he knew what he had to do, or he would be shot like a rat in the grain box. He moved at the same time Carlton did, one man on each side of the board wall, and when Carlton yanked the door open and framed himself in the gray light, Spencer shot him dead center with Cliff Ardmore's revolver.

The hat fell away as the narrow-jawed, round-skulled head went up and back, the large eyes open in surprise, the mouth open in wonder, the narrow ears hearing, perhaps, the blast of the .45 that roared out of the darkness.

Between the time he had turned away from Jerome's body and the time he opened the door, Carlton had shifted the rifle to his left hand and had drawn his pistol with his right. As he fell backward, both weapons clattered on the ground.

Spencer stepped to the doorway and looked down at the body. The one shot had done it, and the only sound in the gray morning came from the movement of horses in the corral. This was what it came to, he thought. Kill or be killed as the rest of the world went on its way.

***

With the ivory-handled revolver tucked away once more in the pocket of his sheepskin coat, Spencer rode into the town of Farlow. Behind him came stepping the dark horse of Wolf Carlton with the body of the stock detective tied across the saddle.

As Spencer came to a stop outside the sheriff's office, the door opened and the portly deputy stepped out and pushed a stained hat down onto his head.

"Who's that you got there?" he asked, lifting his head and showing his stubbled jowls.

Spencer gave a toss of the head in the direction of the dead man. "Take a look, see if you recognize him."

The deputy took careful sidesteps to lower himself from the sidewalk to the street, then walked to the off side of the horse and bent to take a look. "Sumbitch," he said. "It's Wolf Carlton."

"He came after me."

"It really is. It's Wolf Carlton." The deputy looked up and around. "How'd you get him?"

"Up close, nearly face-to-face. Like I said, he came after me."

The deputy shook his head in wonder. "You sure got him."

"It's all yours," said Spencer, holding out the lead rope.

As the deputy turned and took the rope, he seemed to have collected himself. "Where did this happen?"

"Up at the Bates place, same as where the kid Perkins got shot in the back."

"So he came back to get you, you think?"

"I believe so. But he got two surprises. One was that Al Jerome was there, and the other was that he didn't get a shot at me."

"Is that right?" said the deputy. "Where's Al now?"

"He's still up at the Bates place, stone-cold dead. Someone probably needs to go up there."

A distasteful expression crept onto the deputy's face, and the jowls sagged.

"Too much for me all at once," said Spencer. "Two bodies, and a couple of extra horses to boot."

The deputy took an audible, whistling breath through his nose. "I'll pass that along to the sheriff."

Spencer shrugged. "While he's at it, he can go pick up Dick Waltman. He's out in a gully where the A-J riders shoot cull horses."

The deputy looked displeased now, and his face had stiffened. "We'll see what the sheriff thinks of all this."

"Up until now he hasn't had much use for anything I've got to say, but if he wants to ask me questions about any of it, I'll be glad to answer 'em. But I imagine he'll rely on his own theories first."

The deputy's eyes narrowed like pig eyes. "I imagine he *will* want to ask some questions."

"I'll be around," said Spencer. He turned his horse, touched his heel to the flank, and moved down the street. At the corner he turned north onto a side street, where he rode for a block and a half and came to a stop. After tying his horse to the hitching rail, he stepped up onto the sidewalk and went in through a door to a small office.

The clean-shaven, bronze face of Warren Robinson looked up from behind the desk, and the green eyes brushed over the visitor. "Yes?" came the lawyer's voice.

Spencer took out the ivory-handled revolver from his coat pocket and set it on the desk in front of the man. "This is for Mrs. Ardmore," he said. "I was wondering if you could give it to her."

The lawyer did not move his hands as he glanced at the gun. "On the part of whom?" he asked, raising his eyes.

"My name's Spencer Prescott."

The green eyes flickered toward the gun and back. "Any message?"

"Just thanks for her help, and my best regards."

Back out on the main street, a somber silence prevailed. In every third or fourth doorway, someone had come out to watch as he rode by. A hatless man in shirtsleeves and suspenders, a heavyset storekeeper in an apron, a dusky man closed up in a hat and coat—no one spoke as the eyes followed him. Spencer could tell that news traveled fast. He was about to turn south to head out of town when he heard someone call his name. Shifting in the saddle, he saw a compact, dark-featured man who had just come out of a café and stood on the sidewalk with his thumbs hooked in his belt.

Spencer reined the horse around, and as he crossed the street he noted the brown hat with the upturned brim, the full mustache, and the dark neckerchief. The man's beady eyes held on him.

As Spencer drew to a stop, he said, "Hullo, Trask. I'd have thought you were already gone, on your way up to the Big Hole country."

"I thought of it, but I had a small piece of work I wanted to do first."

"Did you get to do it?"

Trask shook his head. "No. And it was what I came here to do. Never got quite the right chance, and now the time's passed." The man's face relaxed. "How about yourself? Are you headed up to the Big Hole country to work with friend Orton?"

"No, not right away, at least. I've got a couple of things to do, so I'll be stickin' around here a while longer."

Trask stepped off the sidewalk and held out his hand. Spencer edged the horse around, and as he leaned in the saddle to shake, Trask said, "So long, Spencer. It's been good to know you." The dark eyes held steady as he said in a lowered voice, "I want to thank you on behalf of my brother."

"Oh," said Spencer, as time seemed to stand still for a moment. Then he found his voice. "I have to admit, all I was thinking of at the time was myself."

"Doesn't matter. It's done now, and the less said, the better."

"Good enough." Spencer took a breath to steady himself. Then he said, "I wish you the best of luck, Trask. When you get to where you're goin', have one for the kid."

Trask nodded, and with a somber cast on his face he said, "At least the son of a bitch didn't get away with it."

***

As Spencer rode into the yard of the Wingate place, the front door of the house opened. Eva stood in the doorway, and he could see her loose, dark hair touching the shoulders of her blue dress. He swung down from the saddle and stood holding his reins as she stepped out onto the doorstep.

"You're back," she said. "That's a good sign in itself." Looking closer, she added, "You look worn out. Are you all right?"

"Oh, I am now. But it wasn't easy."

Her blue eyes had a sparkle as they played over him. "Anything you can tell me about?"

"I imagine so. Maybe not all at once." He saw the worry in her face, and he wanted to put her at ease. "For right now, I'll just say Wolf Carlton won't be bothering anyone anymore."

Her face softened. "That's good to know." Her eyes roved over him again. "I must say, you look exhausted. Have you eaten?"

"I don't remember. It's been a while."

"Well, come in, and I'll fix you something. You can get some rest. Do you have to be anywhere?"

"Um, no. That's part of what I'll get around to telling you. For the moment, though, I thought I'd offer to do something you asked me to do before."

Her face tensed again. "What's that?"

"I can be your rep if you want. Fall roundup's coming up. And while I'm at it, I'll help find the rest of your horses." He glanced at the charred remains next to the corral. "And I'll help you build your stable again."

A bit of color came to her cheeks. "Now, now. You can't do it all at once. And first, you need to eat and get rested up. Come into the house."

"You're right," he said. "I'm dead tired, and I want to say everything at the same time. But I'll say this. I did something."

"That's good. You can tell me about it little by little." She held out her hand as he went up the steps, and together they went into the house.

☐ **YES!**

Sign me up for the Leisure Western Book Club and send my FREE BOOKS! If I choose to stay in the club, I will pay only $14.00* each month, a savings of $9.96!

NAME: _____

ADDRESS: _____

TELEPHONE: _____

EMAIL: _____

☐ I want to pay by credit card.

☐ VISA   ☐ MasterCard   ☐ DISCOVER

ACCOUNT #: _____

EXPIRATION DATE: _____

SIGNATURE: _____

Mail this page along with $2.00 shipping and handling to:
Leisure Western Book Club
PO Box 6640
Wayne, PA 19087
Or fax (must include credit card information) to:
610-995-9274
You can also sign up online at **www.dorchesterpub.com**.
*Plus $2.00 for shipping. Offer open to residents of the U.S. and Canada only.
Canadian residents please call 1-800-481-9191 for pricing information.
If under 18, a parent or guardian must sign. Terms, prices and conditions subject to change. Subscription subject to acceptance. Dorchester Publishing reserves the right to reject any order or cancel any subscription.